CHANGE OF FORM

"You disappeared," declared the Room. "You wrapped yourself in nothing and you disappeared. But before you began to wrap yourself, you changed."

"How could I change?"

"I don't know, but you did. You melted and you took another form, or began to take another form, and then you wrapped yourself."

"And you couldn't sense me? That's why you thought that I had gone away."

"I could not sense you," said the Room. "I could not penetrate the nothingness. . . ."

CLIFFORD D. SIMAK
THE WEREWOLF PRINCIPLE

A BERKLEY MEDALLION BOOK
published by
BERKLEY PUBLISHING CORPORATION

*BERKLEY MEDALLION BOOKS are published by
Berkley Publishing Corporation
200 Madison Avenue
New York, N.Y. 10016*

BERKLEY MEDALLION BOOKS ® TM 757,375

Printed in the United States of America

The creature halted, crouched low against the ground, staring at the tiny points of light that lay ahead, burning softly through the darkness.

The creature whimpered, frightened and uneasy.

The world was much too hot and wet and the darkness was too thick. There was too much and too large vegetation. The atmosphere was in violent motion and the vegetation moaned in agony. Far off in the distance there were vague flarings and flashings of light, which did nothing to illuminate the night, and somewhere far away something was complaining in long, low rumblings. And there was life, far more life than any planet had a right to have—but low and stupid life, some of it scarcely more than biological stirring, tiny bundles of matter that could do no more than react feebly to certain stimuli.

Perhaps, the creature told itself, it should not have tried so hard to break away. Perhaps it should have been content to remain in that nameless place where there had been no being and no sense nor memory of being, but a knowledge, dredged from somewhere, that there was such a state as being. That, and occasional snatches of intelligence, disconnected bits of information, which whetted the struggles to escape, to be a separate agent, to see where it might be and learn why it was there and by what means it might have gotten there.

And now?

It crouched and whimpered.

How could there be so much water in any single place? And so much vegetation and such boisterous agitation of the elements? How could any world be so messy, so flamboyantly un-neat? It was sacrilegious for so much water to be in evidence, running in a stream below this slope of ground, standing in pools and puddles on the very ground. And not only that, but present in the atmosphere, the air filled with driven droplets of it.

What was this fabric which was fastened at its throat and which lay along its back, dragging on the ground, fluttered by the wind? A protection of some sort? Although that didn't seem too likely. It had never needed protection of any sort before. Its coat of silver fur was all that it had needed.

Before? it asked itself. Before what and when? It struggled to think back and there was a dim impression of a crystal land, with cool, dry air, with a dust of snow and sand, with a sky ablaze with many stars and the night as bright as day with the soft, golden shine of moons. And there was a haunting half-memory, blurred all around the edges, of a reaching out into the depths of space to pluck secrets from the stars.

But was this memory or was it fantasy, born of that faceless place from which it had escaped? There was no way of knowing.

The creature extruded a pair of arms and gathered up the fabric off the ground and held it bundled in each arm. The water dripped off it and fell in tiny drops, splashing in the pools of water that lay upon the ground.

Those points of light ahead? Not stars, for they lay too low against the ground and, in any case, there were not any stars. And that, in itself, was unthinkable, for there were always stars.

Cautiously the creature reached out with its mind toward the steady light and there was something there other than the light, a background sense of mineral. Carefully it traced that background and became aware that a block of mineral stood there in the dark, too regular in its shape to be a natural outcrop.

In the distance the mad muttering went on and the flaring of the far-off light ran frightened up the sky.

Should it go on, it wondered, circling wide around the lights? Or should it move in upon them to find out what they were? Or should it, perhaps, retrace its steps in an effort to find once again that emptiness from which it had escaped? Although there was no knowing now where the place might be. When it had broken free, the place had not been there. And since the time of breaking free, it had traveled far.

And where were those other two who also had been in that place of nothingness? Had they broken free as well, or had they stayed behind, sensing, perhaps, the mind-wrenching alienness that lay outside the place? And if they had not escaped, where might they be now?

And not only where, but who?

Why had they never answered? Or had they never heard the question? Perhaps there were not the right conditions in that nameless place for a question to be asked. Strange, the creature thought, to occupy the same space, the same sense of possible-existence, with two other beings and never to be able to communicate with them.

Despite the heat of the night, the creature shivered, deep inside itself.

It could not stay here, it told itself. It could not wander endlessly. It must find a place to shelter. Although where to look for shelter in a world as mad as this was something it had not figured out as yet.

It moved forward slowly, uncertain of itself, uncertain where to go, uncertain what to do.

The lights? it wondered. Should it investigate the lights or should it . . .

The sky exploded. The world was filled to bursting

with a brilliant blueness. The creature, its sight wiped out, all senses canceled, recoiled, and a scream rose keening in its curdled brain. Then the scream cut off and the light was gone and it was back, once again, in the place of nothingness.

2

Rain slapped Andrew Blake across the face and the very earth was trembling with the deadening crash of thunder, the great masses of riven atmosphere rushing together once again, it seemed, just above his head. The air was sharp with the smell of ozone and he could feel cold mud squishing up between his toes.

And how had he gotten here—out in a storm, with no cover for his head and with his robe so soaked it dripped, and without his sandals?

He had stepped out after dinner to have a look at a storm that was boiling up across the western wall of mountains—and here, a second later, he was out in that very storm, or, at least, he hoped it was that very storm.

The wind was moaning in a clump of trees and from the foot of the slope on which he stood he could hear the sound of running water and just across the stream light shone out from windows.

His house, perhaps, he thought, befuddled. Although where his house stood there was no slope and no stream of running water. There were trees, but not so many trees, and there should be other houses.

He put up his hand and scrubbed his head in perplexity and the water he squeezed out of his hair ran down across his face.

The rain, which had slackened for a moment, began beating at him once again with a fresh enthusiasm and he turned toward the house. Not his house, surely, but it was a house and there'd be someone there to tell him where he was and . . .

But tell him where he was! That was insane! A second ago he had been standing on his patio looking at the storm clouds and there had been no rain.

He must be dreaming. Or suffering a hallucination. But the beating rain was not a dream-like rain and the smell of ozone still was in the air—and who had ever found the smell of ozone reeking through a dream?

He started walking toward the house and as he swung his right foot forward, it came in contact with something hard and a blaze of pain flared through his foot and leg.

In agony, he lifted the foot and waved it in the air, jigging on one leg. The pain drained down into the big toe of the lifted foot and it throbbed in agony.

The foot on which he stood slipped in the mud and he sat down suddenly. Mud spatted as his bottom hit the earth. The ground was wet and cold.

He stayed there. He pulled the foot with the injured toe up into his lap and probed blindly—and carefully and tenderly—at the toe.

It was no dream, he knew. In a dream a man would not be so stupid as to stub his toe.

Something had happened. Something, in a second's time, had transported him, all unknowing, perhaps many miles away from where he'd stood on the patio. Had transported him and set him down in the midst of rain and thunder and in a night so dark there was no seeing anything.

He probed at the toe again and it felt a little better.

Carefully, he picked himself up and tried the injured foot. By walking tensed and slightly spraddled, with the toe stretched upward, he could use the leg.

Limping and fumbling and slipping in the mud, he made his way down the slope and across the little stream, which ran ankle deep, then climbed the slope that went up to the house.

Lightning flared along the horizon and for a moment he saw the house silhouetted against the flare, a massive pile, with heavy chimneys and windows set deep, like eyes, into the stone.

A stone house, he thought. An anachronism! A stone house and someone living in it.

He ran into a fence, but without any hurt, for he was moving slowly. He followed it blindly by feel and came to a gate. Beyond the gate three little rectangles of light marked what he took to be the location of a door.

Flat stones lay underneath his feet and he followed them. Near the door he slowed his walk to a cautious shuffle. There might be steps leading to the door and one stubbed toe was all he cared to have.

There were steps. He found them with the still tender toe and stood for a moment, stiff and straight and shuddering, with clenched teeth, until the worst pain ebbed away.

Then he climbed the steps and found the door. He hunted for the signal, but there was no signal—not even a bell or buzzer. He hunted some more and found the knocker.

A knocker? Of course, he told himself, a house like this would have a knocker. A house so deep into the past . . .

A wild fear surged through him. Not space, but time, he wondered. Had he been moved (if he had been moved) not in space, but time?

He lifted the knocker and hammered with it. He waited. There was no sign he had been heard. He hammered once again.

A footstep crunched behind him and a cone of light speared out and caught him. He spun about and the round eye of light held steady, blinding him. Behind the light he sensed the vague figure of a man, the faint outline of a deeper shadow aginst the darkness of the night.

Back of him the door jerked open and light from the inside of the house flooded out and now he saw the man who held the torch, a kilted figure, with a sheepskin jacket and in his other hand a glint of metal that Blake took to be a gun.

The man who had opened the door asked sharply, "What is going on out here?"

"Someone trying to get in, senator," said the man who held the torch. "He must have managed to slip past me."

"He slipped past you," said the senator, "because you were huddled somewhere, hiding from the rain. If you fellows have to play at being guards, I wish you'd do some guarding."

"It was dark," protested the guard, "and he slipped past . . ."

"I don't think he slipped past," said the senator. "He just walked up and banged the knocker. If he'd been trying to sneak in, he'd not have used the knocker. He walked in, like any ordinary citizen, and you didn't see him."

Blake turned slowly to face the man standing in the door.

"I'm sorry, sir," he said. "I didn't know. I didn't mean to raise a ruckus. I just saw the house . . ."

"And that's not all, senator," broke in the guard. "There've been strange things out tonight. Just a while ago I saw a wolf . . ."

"There are no wolves about," said the senator. "There are no wolves at all. There haven't been for a century or more."

"But I saw one," wailed the guard. "There was that big flash of lightning and I saw it, on the hill across the creek."

The senator said to Blake, "I'm sorry to keep you standing with all this bickering. It's no night to be out."

t seems that I am lost," said Blake, fighting to keep his teeth from chattering. "If you'll tell me where I am and point out the way . . ."

"Turn off that light," the senator told the guard, "and get back to your job."

The torch snapped off.

"Wolves, indeed!" said the senator, incensed.

To Blake, he said, "If you'd step in, so I could close the door."

Blake stepped in and the senator closed the door behind him.

Blake looked around him. He stood in a foyer flanked on either side by floor to ceiling doors and in the room beyond a fire burned in a great stone fireplace. The room was crammed with heavy furniture upholstered in bright prints.

The senator stepped past him and stopped to look at him.

"My name is Andrew Blake," said Blake, "and I am afraid I am messing up your floor."

Rain dripping from his robe had made puddles on the floor and a line of wet footprints led from the door to where he stood.

The senator, he saw, was a tall, lean man, with close-clipped white hair and a silvery mustache, beneath which was a firm, straight mouth that had a trap-like quality. He wore a robe of white, with a purple jigsaw motif worked around its edges.

"You look like a drowning rat," said the senator, "if you don't mind my saying so. And you have lost your sandals."

He turned and opened one of the flanking doors to reveal a rack of clothing. Reaching in, he pulled out a thick, brown robe.

"Here," he said, handing it to Blake. "This should serve. Real wool. I take it you are cold."

"Just a bit," said Blake, jaw aching to keep his teeth from chattering.

"Wool will warm you up," said the senator. "You don't see it often. Nothing but synthetics any more. You can get it from a mad man who lives in the Scottish hills. Thinks much the way I do—that there still is virtue in staying close to old realities."

"I am sure you're right," said Blake.

"Take this house," said the senator. "Three centuries old and still as solid as the day that it was built. Built of honest stone and wood. Built by honest workmen. . . ." He looked sharply at Blake. "But here I stand declaiming while you are slowly freezing. Take those stairs off to the right. The first door to the left. That would be my room. You'll find sandals in the closet and I suppose your shorts are soaked as well. . . ."

"I'd suppose they are," said Blake.

"You'll find shorts, anything else that you may need in the dresser. The bath is to the right as you go in. It wouldn't hurt a bit if you took ten minutes of a hot tub. Meanwhile I'll have Elaine rustle up some coffee and I'll break out a bottle of good brandy. . . ."

"You must not put yourself out," said Blake. "You have done too much . . ."

"Not a bit of it," said the senator. "I'm glad that you dropped in."

Clutching the woolen robe, Blake climbed the stairs and went in the first door on the left. Through the door to the right he saw the white gleam of the tub. That hot bath idea was not too bad, he told himself.

He walked into the bath, dropped the brown robe atop a hamper and took off the bedraggled robe he wore and dropped it to the floor.

In surprise he glanced down at himself. He was as naked as a jaybird. Somewhere, somehow, he had lost his shorts.

3

The senator was waiting when Blake came back to the big room with the fire. He was sitting in a chair and on the arm of it perched a dark-haired woman.

"Well," said the senator, "here you are, young man. You told me your name, but I am afraid that it slipped my mind."

"The name is Andrew Blake."

"I'm sorry," said the senator. "My mind does not seem to have the retentive power that it once commanded. This is my daughter, Elaine, and I am Chandler Horton. No doubt, from the yammering of that fool outside, you gathered that I'm a senator."

"I am honored, senator," said Blake, "and, Miss Elaine, very pleased to meet you."

"Blake?" said the girl. "I have heard the name somewhere. Very recently. Tell me, what are you famous for?"

"Why, not a thing," said Blake.

"But it was in all the papers. And you were on dimensino—the live, news part of it. Now I know! You are the man who came back from the stars. . . ."

"You don't say," said the senator, heaving himself from the chair. "How very interesting. Mr. Blake, that chair over there is very comfortable. Place of honor, you might say. Next to the fire and all."

"Daddy," Elaine said to Blake, "has a tendency to wax baronial, or maybe country-squirish, when company drops in. You must never mind him."

"The senator," said Blake, "is a very gracious host."

The senator picked up a decanter and reached for glasses.

"You'll recall," he said, "that I promised you some brandy."

"And," said Elaine, "be careful that you praise it. Even if it gags you. The senator prides himself as a judge of brandy. And if, a little later, you would like some coffee, we can have that, too. I punched the autochef. . . ."

"The chef act up again?" asked the senator.

Elaine shook her head. "Not especially. Got the coffee, just the way I asked—plus fried eggs and bacon."

She looked at Blake. "Want some eggs and bacon? I think they still are warm."

He shook his head. "No, thank you very much."

"The contraption," said the senator, "has been on the fritz for years. One spell, no matter what you dialed, it served up roast beef, rare."

He handed around the glasses and sat down in his chair. "That's why I like this place," he said. "Uncomplicated domicile. It was built three hundred years ago by a man who cared for dignity and had a certain ecological sense that made him build it of native limestone and the timber that grew upon the tract. He did not impose his house upon the habitat; he made it part of it. And, except for the autochef, it has not a single gadget."

"We're old fashioned," said Elaine. "I have always felt that living in a place like this was akin—well, say, to taking up one's residence in a sod shanty in the twentieth century."

"Nevertheless," said Blake, "it has a certain charm. And a sense of security and solidity."

"You are right, it has," said the senator. "Listen to that wind trying to get it. Listen to that rain."

He swirled the brandy in his glass.

"It doesn't fly, of course," he said, "and it won't talk to you. But who wants a house to fly and . . ."

"Daddy!" said Elaine.

"You must excuse me, sir," said the senator. "I have my enthusiasms and I like to talk about them and sometimes I let them run away with me—and there are times, I would suspect, when I have bad manners. My daughter said something about seeing you on dimensino."

"Of course, Daddy," said Elaine. "You never pay attention. You're so wrapped up in the bioengineering hearings that you don't pay attention."

"But, my dear," said the senator, "the hearings are important. The human race must decide before too long what to do with all these planets we are finding. And I tell you that terraforming them is the solution of a lunatic. Think of all the time that it will take and the money that it will swallow up."

"By the way," said Elaine, "I forgot. Mother phoned. She won't be home tonight. She heard about the storm and is staying in New York."

The senator grunted. "Fine. Bad night for traveling. How was London? Did she say?"

"She enjoyed the performance."

"Music hall," the senator explained to Blake. "Revival of an ancient entertainment form. Very primitive, I understand. My wife is taken with it. She is an arty person."

"What a horrible thing to say," said Elaine.

"Not at all," said the senator. "It's the truth. But to get back to this business of bioengineering. Perhaps, Mr. Blake, you have some opinions."

"No," said Blake, "I can't say that I have. I find myself somewhat out of touch."

"Out of touch? Oh, yes, I suppose you would be. This business of the stars. I recall the story now. Encapsulated, as I remember it, and found by some asteroid miners. What system was it, now?"

"Out in the Antares neighborhood. A small star—just a number, not a name. But I remember none of that.

They waited to revive me until I was brought to Washington."

"And you remember nothing?"

"Not a thing," said Blake. "My life began, so far as I'm concerned, less than a month ago. I don't know who I am or . . ."

"But you have a name."

"A mere convenience," said Blake. "One that I picked out. John Smith would have done as well. It seems a man must have a name."

"But, as I recall it, you had background knowledge."

"Yes—and that is a strange thing. A knowledge of the earth and of its people and of its ways, but in many ways hopelessly outdated. I continually am astounded. I stumble into customs and beliefs and words that are unfamiliar to me."

Elaine said, quietly, "You don't need to talk about it. We hadn't meant to pry."

"I don't mind," Blake told her. "I've accepted the situation. It's a strange position to be in, but some day I may know. It may come back to me—who I am and where I came from and when. And what happened out there. At the moment, as you may understand, I am considerably confused. Everyone, however, has been considerate. I was given a house to live in. And I've not been bothered. It's in a little village. . . ."

"This village?" asked the senator. "Nearby, I presume."

"I don't actually know," said Blake. "Something funny happened to me. I don't know where I am. The village is called Middleton."

"That's just down the valley," said the senator. "Not five miles from here. It would seem that we are neighbors."

"I went out after dinner," Blake told them. "I was on the patio, looking toward the mountains. A storm was coming up. Big black clouds and lightning, but still a good ways off. And then, suddenly, I was on the hill across the creek from this place and the rain was coming down and I was soaked . . ."

He stopped and set down his brandy glass, carefully, on the hearth. He stared from one to the other of them.

"That's the way it was," he said. "I know that it sounds wild."

"It sounds impossible," said the senator.

"I am sure it does," said Blake. "And there was not only space, but time, as well, involved. Not only did I find myself some miles away from where I had been standing, but it was night and when I stepped out on the patio dusk had just begun to fall."

"I am sorry," said the senator, "that the stupid guard threw the light on you. Finding yourself here must have been shock enough. I don't ask for guards. I don't even want them. But Geneva insists that all senators must be guarded. I don't know exactly why. There is no one, I am sure, thirsting for our blood. Finally, after many years, Earth is at least part-way civilized."

"There is this bioengineering business," said Elaine. "Feelings do run high."

"Nothing is involved," said the senator, "except a determination of policy. There is no reason. . . ."

"But there is," she said. "All the Bible Belt fanatics, all the arch conservatives, all the prissy conventionists are dead set against it."

She turned toward Blake. "Wouldn't you know," she said, "that the senator, who lives in a house built three hundred years ago and brags about there being not a single gadget in it . . ."

"The chef," said the senator. "You forget the chef."

She ignored him. "And brags about not a single gadget in it, would align himself with the wild-eyed bunch, with the arch-progressives, with the far-out gang?"

The senator sputtered. "Not a thing far-out about it. It just makes common sense. It will cost trillions of dollars to terraform a single planet. At a cost much more reasonable, and in a fraction of the time required, we can engineer a human race that could live upon that planet. Instead of changing the planet to fit the man, we change the man to fit the planet. . . ."

"That's exactly the point," said Elaine. "That's the point your opponents have been making. Change the man—that's the thing that sticks fast inside their craws. When you got through, this thing that would live upon another planet would not be a man."

"It might not look like one," said the senator, "but it still would be a man."

She said to Blake, "You understand, of course, that I'm not against the senator. But there are times when it's terribly hard to make him realize what he's up against."

"My daughter," said the senator, "plays my devil's advocate and at times it is a service. But in this instance there is no particular need. I know the bitterness of the opposition."

He lifted the decanter.

Blake shook his head. "If there is some way I can get back home. It has been quite a night."

"You could stay the night with us."

"Thank you, senator, but if there is some way . . ."

"Certainly," said the senator. "One of the guards can take you. We had better use the ground car. Bad night for a floater."

"I would appreciate it."

"It'll give one of the guards a chance to be of use," said the senator. "Driving you home, they won't be seeing wolves. By the way, when you were out there, you didn't see a wolf?"

"No," said Blake, "I didn't see a wolf."

4

Michael Daniels stood at the window and watched the ground crew at the Riverside development across the boulevard bring the houses in. The black foundation blocks gleamed wetly in the night and the Potomac, a quarter mile beyond, was a sheet of inky darkness that picked up and reflected back the gleam of the landing lights.

Slowly, one by one, the houses came lumbering down out of the cloud-fogged sky, to stop above their assigned foundations, hovering there and moving slowly and deliberately to square their landing grids with the foundation patterns.

Patients coming in, thought Daniels. Or, perhaps, staff members returning from a holiday. Although there might be, as well, others who were unconnected with the hospital, either as patient or as staff. The town was crowded, with the regional bioengineering hearings due to open in a day or two. Space was at a premium and migrating houses were being squeezed in wherever accommodations could be found.

Far across the river, somewhere over Old Virginia, its lights dimmed by fog and drizzle, a ship was coming in, heading for a landing at the spaceport.

Following its flight, Daniels speculated from what far star it might have come. And how long away from home? He smiled ruefully to himself. These were questions that he always asked—a holdover from a boyhood when he had held the hard determination that some day he would travel to the stars.

But in this, he knew, he was not unusual. Every boy, these days, dreamed of going to the stars.

Streams of moisture ran in jagged patterns down the smooth glass of the windows and beyond the windows the houses still came floating in, filling up the few foundations still available. A few ground cars went sliding smoothly along the boulevard, the cushions of air on which they rode throwing out a wide spray of water from the dampened surface. It was too foul a night, he told himself, for many floaters to be out.

He should be getting home, he knew. He should have left long ago. The kids would be in bed by now, but Cheryl would be waiting up for him.

To the east, almost beyond the angle of his vision, glowing by reflected light, he could see the ghost-like whiteness of the shaft that rose beside the river in honor of the first astronauts, who had gone out more than five hundred years ago to circle earth in space, boosted there by the raw, brute power of chemical reaction.

Washington, he thought, a town of mouldering buildings, and filled with monuments—a tangle of marble and of granite, and thick with the moss of old associations, its metal and its stone veneered with the patina of ancient memories and with the aura of once-great power still hanging over it. Once the national capital of an old republic, now no more than a seat of provincial government, it still held an air of greatness draped about it like a cloak.

And it was best, he thought, at a time like this, when a soft, wet night had fallen over it, creating an illusive background through which old ghosts could move.

The hushed sounds of a hospital at night whispered in the room—the soft padding of a nurse going down the corridor, the muted rumble of a cart, the low buzzing of a call bell at the station just across the hall.

Behind him someone opened the door. Daniels swung around.

"Good evening, Gordy," he said.

Gordon Barnes, a resident, grinned at him. "I thought you'd be gone by now," he said.

"Just about to. I was going over that report."

He gestured at the table in the center of the room.

Barnes picked up the file of papers and glanced at it.

"Andrew Blake," he said. "An intriguing piece of business."

Daniels shook his head in puzzlement. "More than intriguing," he declared. "It just isn't possible. How old would you take Blake to be? By just looking at him."

"Not more than thirty, Mike. Of course we know he could be a couple of hundred, chronologically."

"If he were thirty, you'd expect some deterioration, wouldn't you? The body begins wearing out early in the twenties. From there it goes progressively downhill, heading toward old age."

"I know," said Barnes. "But not this Blake, I take it."

"Perfect," said Daniels. "A perfect specimen. Youthful. More than youthful. Not a blemish. Not a weakness."

"And no evidence of who he really is?"

Daniels shook his head. "Space Administration has gone through the records with a fine-toothed comb. He could be any one of thousands of people. Within just the last two centuries, several dozen ships have simply disappeared. Went out and no more heard of them. He could be any one of the people who were aboard those ships."

"Someone froze him," said Barnes, "and stuck him in the capsule. Could that be a clue of some sort?"

"You mean someone who was so important that someone else took a chance at saving him?"

"Something like that."

"It doesn't make sense," said Daniels. "Even if they did, it still is a bit too sticky. Fire a man out into space and what are the chances he'll be found again? A billion to one? A trillion to one? I don't know. Space is big and empty."

"But Blake was found."

"Yes, I know. His capsule floated into a solar system that had been colonized less than a hundred years ago and a gang of asteroid miners found him. The capsule had taken up an orbit around an asteroid and they saw it flashing in the sun and got curious. Too much flash to it. Had dreams of finding a monstrous diamond or something. A few years longer and he would have crashed on the asteroid. Try to figure out those odds."

Barnes laid the folder back on the table and walked over to the window to stand beside Daniels.

"I agree with you," he said. "It makes little sense. The odds keep working for the man. Even after he was found, someone could have broken open the capsule. They knew there was a man in there. The capsule was transparent; they could see him. Someone could have gotten the wild idea of trying to thaw him out and resuscitating him. It could have been worth their while. Who knows, he might have some information that it would be worth their having."

"Fat lot of good it would have done," said Daniels. "That's another thing. Blake's mind was blank except for a general human background—the kind of general background a man could have gotten only on the Earth. He had the language and the human outlook and the sort of basic information that a man who lived two hundred years ago would have stored away. But that was all. No slightest memory of what might have happened to him or who he was or where he might have come from."

"There is no question that he originally came from Earth? Not from one of the stellar colonies?"

"There doesn't seem to be. He knew where and what Washington was once we had revived him. But to him it still was the capital of the United States. And there were a lot of other things, as well, that only an Earthman would have known. As you can well imagine, we ran him through quite a bunch of tests."

"How is he getting along?"

"Apparently all right. I haven't heard from him. He's in a little community west of here. Out in the mountains. He thought, and I thought, he should get some resting time. Time just to take it easy. That might give him a chance to do some thinking, do some probing back. By now he may be beginning to recall who and what he was. I didn't suggest it—I didn't want to put any burden on him. But I'd think it would be natural that he might. He was a bit upset about it all."

"And if he does, he'll tell you?"

"I don't know," said Daniels. "I would hope he might. But I kept no strings on him. I didn't think it wise. Let him do it on his own. If he gets in trouble, I think he'll get in touch."

5

Blake stood on the patio and watched the red tail lights of the ground car recede swiftly up the street.

The rain had stopped and through the scudding clouds a few stars could be seen. Up and down the street, the houses stood dark, with only the yard lights burning. In his own house a light was burning in the entry hall—a sign that the house was waiting up for him. To the west the mountains humped, a darker blot against the sky.

The wind that came cutting out of the northwest was cold and Blake pulled the brown wool of the robe tight about his chest and shucked it up about his ears.

Hunched in the robe, Blake turned and crossed the patio, mounted the short three steps up to the door. The door came open and he stepped inside.

"Good evening, sir," said the House, and then, in a tone of reprimand, "it appears you were detained."

"Something happened to me," said Blake. "Would you have any idea what it might have been?"

"You left the patio," said the House, disgusted that he should expect further information from it. "You are aware, of course, that our concern does not extend beyond the patio."

"Yes," mumbled Blake. "I am aware of that."

"You should have let us know you were going out," the House said, sternly. "You could have made arrangements to keep in touch with us. We would have provided clothing that was appropriate. As it is, I see you have come back with clothing different than you were wearing when you left."

"A friend loaned it to me," said Blake.

"While you were gone," the House told him, "a message came for you. It is on the P.G."

The postalgraph machine stood to one side of the entry way. Blake stepped over to it and pulled out the sheet of paper projecting from its face. The message was written in precise, bold hand and was short and formal. It read:

If Mr. Andrew Blake should find it convenient to contact Mr. Ryan Wilson at the town of Willow Grove, he might learn something to his great advantage.

Blake held the sheet gingerly between his fingers. It was incredible, he thought. It smelled of melodrama.

"Willow Grove?" he asked.

Said the House, "We'll look it up."

"If you please," said Blake.

"A bath can be ready in a moment," said the House, "if that is what you wish?"

"Food also can be ready soon," yelled the Kitchen. "What does the master wish?"

"I think," said Blake, "I would like some food. How about some ham and eggs and a slice or two of toast."

"Something else could be made as easily," said the Kitchen. "Welsh rarebit? Lobster thermidor?"

"Ham and eggs," said Blake.

"How about the decor?" asked the House. "We have had the present one for an unseemly length of time."

"No," Blake told it, wearily, "leave it as it is. Leave the decor be. It doesn't really matter."

"Of course it matters," the House said, tartly. "There is such a thing as . . ."

"Just leave it be," said Blake.

"As you wish, master," said the House.

"Food first," said Blake, "then the bath, then off to bed. It's been quite a day."

"And the message?"

"Forget about it now. We'll think of it tomorrow."

"The town of Willow Grove," said the House, "is northwest of here. Fifty-seven miles. We looked it up."

Blake walked across the living room into the dining room and sat down at the table.

"You have to come and get it," wailed the Kitchen. "I can't bring it to you."

"I know that," said Blake. "Tell me when it's ready."

"But you're sitting at the table!"

"The man has a right to sit wherever he may wish," stormed the House.

"Yes, sir," said the Kitchen.

The House relapsed into silence and Blake sat in the chair, bone tired.

The wallpaper of the room, he saw, had been animated. Although, come to think of it, it wasn't really wallpaper. The House had pointed that out to him the day he had arrived.

There were, he thought, so many new things, that he often was confused.

It was a woodland scene, interspersed with meadows, and with a brook that ran through woods and meadow. A rabbit came hopping deliberately along. It stopped beside a clump of clover and settled down to nibble at the blossoms. Its ears went back and forth and it scratched itself, holding its head to one side and hitting gentle strokes with a ponderous hind leg. The brook sparkled in the sunlight as it ran down a tiny rapids and there were flecks of foam and fallen leaves riding on its surface. A bird flew across the scene and landed in a tree. It raised its head and sang, but there was no sound. One could tell that it was singing by the trembling of its throat.

"Would you like the sound turned on?" asked the Dining Room.

"No, thank you. I don't believe I would. I want just to sit and rest. Some other time, perhaps."

To sit and rest and think—to get it figured out. To try to find what had happened to him and how it might have happened, and why, of course, as well. And to determine who or what he was, what he had been and what he might be now. It all was, he thought, a nightmare happening while he was wide awake.

Although when morning came, it might be all right again, it might seem all right again. The sun would be shining then and the world be bright. He'd go out for a walk and talk with some of the neighbors up and down the street and it would be all right. Perhaps if he just forgot about it, brushed it from his mind—that, perhaps, would be the best way to handle it. It might not happen again and if it didn't happen, there'd be no need to worry.

He stirred uneasily in the chair.

"What time is it?" he asked. "How long was I gone?"

"It is almost two o'clock," said the House. "You went away at eight or very shortly after."

Six hours, he thought, and he could account for two of them at most. What had happened in those other four hours and why could he not recall them? For that matter, why could he not recall the time when he had been in space and the time before he was in space? Why must his life start with that moment he had opened his eyes in a hospital bed in Washington? There had been another time, there had been other years. He once had held a name and history—and what had happened to blot it all away?

The rabbit finished its munching of the clover and went hopping off. The bird sat on the limb, no longer singing. A squirrel ran head-first down a tree trunk, halted two feet above the ground, spun like a flash and scurried up again. It reached a limb and ran out on it for a ways, then halted, poised, its tail jerking in excitement.

Like sitting in a window, Blake thought, gazing out at the woodland scene—for there was no flatness to it. It had depth and perspective and the color of the landscape was no painted color, but the color one would know if he had looked upon an actual scene.

The House still puzzled and disturbed him, at times made him uncomfortable. There was nothing in his background memory that had prepared him for anything like this. Although he could recall, in that misty time before complete forgetfulness closed down, that someone (whose name he could not recall) had cracked the enigma of gravity and that functioning solar power had been commonplace.

But while the house was energized by its solar power plant and was mobile by virtue of its anti-gravity apparatus, it was much more than that. It was a robot—a robot with a good-servant complex built into it, and at times, it seemed, almost a mother complex. It took care of the people that it housed. It had their welfare firmly fixed in its computer-mind. It talked with them and served them, it reminded them and bullied them and nagged at them and coddled them. It was house and servant and companion all rolled into one. A man, Blake told himself, in time could come to look upon his house as a loyal and loving friend.

The House did everything for you. It fed you and did the washing, it tucked you into bed, and given half a chance, it would wipe your nose. It watched over you and anticipated every single wish and sometimes was objectionable in its wish to do too much. It dreamed up things that it imagined you might like—like the animated wallpaper (oops, not wallpaper!) with the rabbit and the singing bird.

But, Blake told himself, it took some getting used to. Maybe not for someone who had lived his life with it. But come back from the stars, God knows from where or when, and be thrown into a house like this—then it took some getting used to.

"Come and get it!" bawled the Kitchen. "Ham and eggs are ready!"

6

It came alive humped in a place it had never sensed before—a strange enclosure inhabited by artifacts made mostly out of wood, although there was some metal and some fabric.

It reacted instantly. It snapped out its defenses and blotted out the place. It built itself into a pyramid, which was a solid state of being, and constructed about itself a sphere of isolation.

It tested for the energy that it would need to power its life and spark its mentality and the energy was there, a surging tide of energy deriving from some source it could not detect.

It found that now it could cogitate. Its mental processes were bright and clear, its logic like a knife. No longer was there a dream-like quality in its thinking. The unquestioned pyramidal body mass gave it stability and a theater in which its mind could operate.

It directed its thinking toward the solution of what had happened to it—how, after an unknown period of time, during which it had only been marginally operative, if even marginally, it suddenly had come free and whole and efficient once again.

It sought for a beginning and there was no beginning, or, perhaps, only a beginning so hazed and indistinct that it could not be sure. It sought and dug and hunted, sniffing through the dark tunnels of its mind, and there was no beginning it could peg down tight and solid.

Although that, it told itself, was of no great consequence, for a beginning might not be essential. Had there
ever, it wondered, been a beginning or had it always
hunted thus, scrabbling in its mental mazes for an anchor
post? A beginning, of course, was not necessary, nor was
an ending necessary, either, but somewhere, somehow,
there must be an approximation of a beginning and an
end.

Perhaps the question, rather, was had there been a
past, and it was certain there must have been a past, for
its mind was packed with the floating foam of flotsam
that came drifting from the past—background bits of information, like the background radiation that could be
found upon a planet. It tried to patch the foam into a
pattern and no pattern came, for there was no way that
the bits of information could be made to fit into one another.

The data, it thought in panic—once there had been
data. It was sure there had been data. Once there had
been something with which its mind could work. And the
data might still be present, but masked or under cover,
appearing only in spots and patches, and some of it irrel-
evant, although one could not be sure, for there did not
seem to be enough of it to establish relevance.

It squatted in its pyramidal form and listened to the
empty thrumming of its mind, a polished able mind, but
without the facts to work on—a mind that was running
wild and empty, with no accomplishment.

It sought again in the jumbled tangle of the bits and
pieces that floated from the past and it found the impression of a rocky, hostile land, out of the rock of which
reared up a massive cylinder, black as the rock itself,
soaring up into the greyness of the sky until it made one
dizzy to try to follow it. And within the cylinder, it knew,
was something that defied all imagination, something so

great and wondrous that the mind recoiled at the thinking of it.

It sought for the meaning, for some hint or recognition, but there was nothing but the image of the black and rocky land and the blackness and the bleakness of the cylinder that came soaring out of it.

Reluctantly, it let the picture go and dredged for another piece and this time it was a flowery glen that opened on a meadow and the meadow was wild with the thousand hues of a billion blooming flowers. The sound of music shivered in the air and there were living things that romped among the flowers and again there was a meaning here, it knew, but there was no clue that it could find which would allow it to approach the meaning.

There had been another, once. There had been another being and it had been this being which had snared and held the pictures and transmitted them—and not the pictures only, but the data that went with them. And still the pictures were filed within the mind, although jumbled all together, but the data that was tied in with them had somehow disappeared.

It crouched lower and deeper and more massively into its pyramidal form and within its brain the emptiness and the chaos ached and it tried gropingly to go back into its twilit past to find that other creature which had supplied the picture and the data.

But there was nothing to be found. There was no way to reach out and touch this other one. And it wept in loneliness, deep inside itself, without tears or sobbing, for it was not equipped for either tears or sobbing.

And in the bareness of its grief it drove back deeper into time and found a time when there had been no creature, when it still had worked with data and with abstract pictures based upon the data, but there had been no color in either the data or the concept and the pictures so

erected had been stiff and prim and at times even terrifying.

There was no use, it thought. There was no use of
trying. It still was inefficient, it was only half itself, and it
could not function properly because it lacked the material
to perform its function. It sensed the blackness drifting in
upon it and it did not fight against it. It stayed and waited
and let the blackness come.

7

Blake awoke and the Room was screaming at him.

"Where did you go?" it screamed at him. "Where did you go? What happened to you?"

He was sitting on the floor in the center of the room, sitting with his legs pulled underneath him. And it was not right, for he should have been in bed.

The Room began again. "Where did you go?" it bellowed. "What happened to you? What did . . ."

"Oh, shut up," said Blake.

The Room shut up.

Morning sunlight was streaming through the window and somewhere outside a bird was singing. The room was ordinary. Nothing had been changed. It was all exactly as he remembered it when he had gone to bed.

"Now tell me," he said. "Exactly what did happen?"

"You went away!" wailed the Room. "And you built a wall around you . . ."

"A wall!"

"A nothingness," said the Room. "A blob of nothingness. You filled me with a cloud of nothingness."

Blake said, "You are crazy. How could I do a thing like that?"

But even as he said the words, he knew that the Room was right. The Room could only report the phenomenon that it had sensed. It had no such thing as imagination. It was only a machine, although a sophisticated one, and in its experience there was no such thing as superstition, or myth or fairy tale.

"You disappeared," declared the Room. "You wrapped yourself in nothing and you disappeared. But before you began to wrap yourself, you changed."

"How could I change?"

"I don't know, but you did. You melted and you took another form, or began to take another form, and then you wrapped yourself."

"And you couldn't sense me? That's why you thought that I had gone away."

"I could not sense you," said the Room. "I could not penetrate the nothingness."

"This nothingness?"

"Just nothingness," said the Room. "I could not analyze it."

Blake picked himself up off the floor, reached for the pair of shorts he had dropped upon the floor when he'd gotten into bed the night before. He pulled them on and picked up the robe draped across a chair back.

He lifted it and it was heavy and it was brown and it was wool—and suddenly he remembered the night before, the strange stone house and the senator and his daughter.

You changed, the Room had said. You changed and built around yourself a shell of nothingness. But he had no memory of it, not a whisper of a memory.

Nor had he any memory of what had happened the night before in that interval between when he'd walked on the patio and the moment he had found himself standing in the storm, a good five miles from home.

My God, he asked himself, what is going on?

He sat down suddenly on the bed, the robe draped across his knees.

"Room," he asked, "you're sure?"

"I am certain," said the Room.

"Any speculation?"

"You know very well," the Room said, stiffly, "that I would not speculate."

"No, of course you wouldn't."

"Speculation," said the Room, "is illogical."

"You're right, of course," said Blake.

He rose and put on the robe and moved toward the door.

"You have nothing more to say?" the Room asked, disapprovingly.

"What could I say?" asked Blake. "You know more of it than I do."

He went out the door and along the balcony. As he reached the stairway, the House greeted him in its usual cheery morning fashion.

"Good morning, sir," it sang. "The sun is up and bright. The storm is over and there are no clouds. The forecast is for fair and warm. The present temperature is 49 and before the day is over, it will reach more than 60. A beautiful autumn day has dawned and everything looks fine. Do you have any preferences, sir? How about the decor? How about the furniture? How about some music?"

"Ask him," the Kitchen bellowed, "what he wants to eat."

"And, also," said the House, "what do you want to eat?"

"How about some oatmeal?"

"Oatmeal!" wailed the kitchen. "It is always oatmeal. Or it's ham and eggs. Or it's pancakes. Just for once, why not something special? Why not . . ."

"Oatmeal," Blake insisted.

"The man wants oatmeal," said the House.

"O.K.," said the Kitchen, beaten. "One oatmeal coming up."

"You must not mind the Kitchen," said the House. "It

labors under a very great frustration. It has all these fancy recipes programmed into its cores and it's really very good at them, but it almost never gets a chance to use a single one of them. Sometime, sir, just for the hell of it, why don't you let the Kitchen . . ."

"Oatmeal," said Blake.

"Oh, very well, sir. The morning paper is in the P.G. tray. But there's not much news this morning."

"If you don't mind," said Blake, "I'll take a look myself."

"Quite, sir. As you wish, sir. I was only attempting to be informative."

"Just try," said Blake, "not to overdo it."

"Sorry, sir," said the House. "I will watch myself."

In the entry hall he picked up the paper and tucked it underneath his arm. He walked to a side window to look out.

The house next door was gone. The platform stood empty.

"They left this morning," said the House. "About an hour ago. A short vacation trip, I gather. We all are glad . . ."

"We?"

"Why, yes. All the other houses, sir. We are glad they're only to be gone for a short time and will becoming back again. They are such good neighbors, sir."

"You seem to know a lot about them. I haven't more than spoken to them."

"Oh," said the House, "not the people, sir. I wasn't talking of the people. It was the house itself I was thinking of."

"You houses, then, consider yourself neighbors."

"Why, of course we do. We visit among ourselves. We talk back and forth."

"Just exchanging information."

"Naturally," said the House. "But now about the decor."

"It's all right as it is."

"It's been this way for weeks."

"Well," Blake said, thoughtfully, "you might do something about that wallpaper in the dining room."

"It's not the wallpaper, sir."

"I know it's not. The point I want to make is that I'm getting a little bored watching that rabbit nibble clover."

"What would you like instead?"

"Anything you like. Just so it has no rabbits in it."

"But, sir, we can work out some thousands of combinations."

"Anything you like," said Blake, "but be sure there are no rabbits."

He turned from the window and went into the dining room. Eyes stared out at him from the walls—thousands of eyes, eyes without a single face, eyes plucked from many faces and plastered on the walls. And while there were some of them that went in pairs, there were others that stood alone. And every eye was staring straight at him.

There were baby-blue eyes, with the look of wistful innocence, and the bloodshot eyes that glared with fearsomeness, the lecherous eye, the dimmed and rheumy eye of the very old. And they all knew him, knew who he was, and they stared at him in a horribly personal manner and if there had been mouths to go with the eyes they all would be talking at him, screaming at him, mouthing at him.

"House!" he screamed.

"What is the matter, sir?"

"These eyes!"

"But you said, sir, anything but rabbits. I thought the eyes were quite a novel . . ."

"Get them out of here!" howled Blake.

The eyes went away and in their place a beach led down to a seashore. The white sand ran down to the surging waves that came beating in and on a distant headland; scraggly, weather-beaten trees leaned against the wind. Above the water birds were flying, screaming as they flew. And within the room was the smell of salt and sand.

"Better?" asked the House.

"Yes," said Blake, "much better. Thank you very much."

He sat entranced, staring out upon the scene. It was, he told himself, as if he sat upon the beach.

"We put in the sound and smell," said the House. "We can add the wind as well."

"No," said Blake. "This is quite enough."

The waves came thundering in and the birds flew crying over them and the great black clouds were rolling up the sky. Was there anything, he wondered, that the House could not reproduce upon that wall? Thousands of combinations, the House had said. A man could sit here and stare out upon any scene he wished.

A house, he thought. What was a house? How had it evolved?

First, in mankind's dim beginning, no more than a shelter to shield a man against the wind and rain, a place in which to huddle, a place for one to hide. And that, basically, still might be its definition, but now a man did more than hide and huddle; a house was a place to live. Perhaps the day might come, in some future time, when a man no more would leave his house, but live out his life inside it, never venturing out of doors, with no need or urge to venture.

That day, he told himself, might be nearer than one thought. For a house no longer was a shelter merely or a simple place to live. It was a companion and a servant and within its walls was all that one might need.

Off the living room stood the tiny room that housed the dimensino, the logical expansion and development of the TV he had known two hundred years ago. But now it was no longer something that one watched and listened to, but something one experienced. A piece of imagery, he thought, with this stretch of seacoast that lay upon the wall. Once in that room, with the set turned on, one entered into the action and the sense of the entertainment form. Not only was one surrounded and caught up by the sound, the smell, the taste, the temperature, the feel of what was going on, but in some subtle way became a sympathetic and an understanding part of the action and emotion that the room portrayed.

And opposite the dimensino, in a corner of the living area, was the library that contained within the simplicity of its electronic being all the literature that still survived from man's long history. Here one could dial and select all the extant thoughts and hopes of every human being who had ever put down words, trying to capture on a sheet of paper the ferment of experience and of feeling and conviction which welled inside the brain.

It was—this house—a far cry from two centuries ago, a structure and an institution which must be wondered at. And it was not finished yet. In another two centuries there might be as many changes and refinements as there had been in the last two hundred years. Would there ever be an end, he wondered, to the concept of the house?

He took the paper from underneath his arm and opened it. The House had been right, he saw. There was little news.

Three men had been newly nominated for the Intelligence Depository, to join all those other selected humans whose thoughts and personalities, knowledge and intelligence, had over the last three hundred years been impressed into the massive mind bank which carried in its cores the amassed beliefs and thoughts of the world's most intellectual humans. The North American weather-modification project finally had been referred for review to the supreme court in Rome. The squabble over the shrimp herds off the coast of Florida still was going on. A survey and exploration ship finally had touched down at Moscow, after being gone for ten years and given up for lost. And the regional hearings on the biological engineering proposal would begin in Washington tomorrow.

The biological engineering story carried with it two one-column cuts, one of Senator Chandler Horton and the other of Senator Solomon Stone.

Blake folded the paper and settled down to read.

WASHINGTON, NORTH AMERICA—The two senators of North America will square off on the proposal for the much-argued program of biological engineering as the regional hearing on the matter opens here tomorrow. Political fireworks are expected. No proposal in recent years has so seized the public imagination and no matter of greater controversy exists in the world today.

North America's two senators find themselves diametrically opposed, as indeed they have been opposed throughout the greater part of their political careers. Senator Chandler Horton has taken a firm stand in approval of the proposal, which will be submitted at the beginning of next year to a worldwide referendum. Senator Solomon Stone is as firmly opposed to it.

That these two men should find themselves an opposite sides of the fence is nothing new. But the political significance of this issue goes deeper because of the so-called Unanimous Consent rule, whereby, on special issues of this sort, submitted to universal referendum, the mandate of the voters must be unanimously approved on the floor of the World Senate at Geneva.

Thus, should the vote be favorable, Senator Stone would be required to stipulate that he would vote to confirm the measure on the senate floor. Failing in this, he would be bound to step aside by resignation of his seat. In this case a special election would be held to fill the vacancy caused by his resignation. Only candidates who made prior pledges to uphold the measure would be eligible to file for the special election.

If the referendum should go against the measure, Senator Horton would find himself in a similar position.

In the past, when this situation obtained, certain senators have retained their seats by voting for the proposals which they had opposed. This would not be the case, most observers agree, with either Stone or Horton. Both have placed their political lives and reputations squarely on the line. Their political philosophies are at opposite poles of the spectrum and over the years their personal antipathy toward one another has become a senatorial legend. It is not believed, at this late date, that either. . . .

"You'll pardon me, sir," said the House, "but Upstairs informs me that a strange thing happened to you. You are all right, I trust."

Blake looked up from the paper.

"Yes," he said. "I am all right."

"But might it not," the House insisted, "be a good idea for you to see a medic."

Blake laid down the paper and opened his mouth— then closed it firmly. After all, officious as it might be, the House had his good at heart. It was a servo-mechanism and its sole thought and purpose was to serve the human that it sheltered.

"Perhaps," he said, "you're right."

For there was no question that there was something

wrong. Within less than twenty-four hours something strange had happened to him twice.

"There was that doctor in Washington," he said. "At the hospital where they took me to revive me. I think his name was Daniels."

"Dr. Michael Daniels," said the House.

"You know his name?"

"Our file on you," said the House, "is really quite complete. How, otherwise, could we serve you as we are supposed to do?"

"You have his number, then. You could call him."

"Why, of course. If you wish me to."

"If you please," said Blake.

He laid the paper on the table and got up and walked into the living room. He sat down before the phone and the small vision panel lit up, flickering.

"In just a moment, sir," said the House.

The panel cleared and in it were the head and shoulders of Dr. Michael Daniels.

"Andrew Blake. You remember me?"

"Certainly I remember you," said Daniels. "I was wondering just last night about you. How you were getting on."

"Physically, I'm O.K.," said Blake. "But I've been having—well, until you find otherwise, I suppose you'd call them hallucinations."

"But you don't think they are hallucinations."

"I'm fairly sure they're not," said Blake.

"Could you come in?" asked Daniels. "I'd like to check you out."

"I'd be glad to come in, doctor."

"Washington's bulging at the seams," said Daniels. "Everything is full. People coming in for the bioengineering show. There's a housing lot just across the street from us. Can you wait while I make a check?"

"I can wait," said Blake.

Daniels' face disappeared and the fuzzy blur of an office, out of focus, danced vaguely on the screen.

Kitchen's voice bellowed: "One oatmeal cooked and waiting. Also toast. Also eggs and bacon. Also a pot of coffee."

"Master's busy on the phone," said the House, disapprovingly. "And all he ordered was the oatmeal."

"He might change his mind," said Kitchen. "Oatmeal might not be enough. He might be hungrier than he thought. You would not want it said that we were starving him."

Daniels came back into the panel.

"Thanks for waiting," he said. "I checked. There is no space available right now. There'll be one foundation in the morning. I reserved it for you. Can it wait that long?"

"I think it can," said Blake. "I only want to talk with you."

"We could talk right now."

Blake shook his head.

"I understand," said Daniels. "See you tomorrow, then. Let's say one o'clock. What are your plans today?"

"I haven't any plans."

"Why don't you go fishing. Get your mind off things. Occupy yourself. Are you a fisherman?"

"I don't know. I hadn't thought about it. It seems to me I may have been. The sport has a familiar sound to it."

"Things still dribbling back," said Daniels. "Still remembering . . ."

"Not remembering. Just the background. Pieces of it falling into shape every now and then. But it doesn't really tell me anything. Someone mentions something or I read of something and it's suddenly familiar, a statement or a fact or a situation that I can accept. Something that I've known or encountered at some former time, but not when or how or under what conditions I encountered it."

"I'd give a lot," said Daniels, "for us to get a clue or two from that background of yours."

"I simply live with it," said Blake. "That's the only way I can get along."

"It's the only sensible approach," Daniels agreed. "You have a good day fishing and I'll see you tomorrow. Seems to me there are some trout streams out in your locality. Hunt up one of them."

"Thank you, doctor."

The phone clicked off and the screen went blank. Blake swung around.

"As soon as you've finished breakfast," said the House, "we'll have the floater waiting on the patio. You'll find fishing tackle in the back bedroom, which is used as a sort of store house, and Kitchen will fix you up a lunch. In the meantime I'll look up a good trout stream and have directions for you and . . ."

"Cut out that yammering!" howled the Kitchen. "Breakfast is getting cold."

8

The water foamed through the jam of fallen trees and brush that in some earlier springtime flood had been caught between the clump of birch and the high cut bank that marked a sharp curve in the stream—foamed through the barrier and then smoothed out in a quiet, dark pool.

Carefully Blake guided the chair-like floater to the ground at one end of the barrier, close to the clump of birch, snapped off the gravity field as it came to rest. For a moment he sat in the chair unmoving, listening to the churning of the water, charmed by the deep quietness of the pool. Ahead of him the mountain range lifted in the sky.

Finally he got out of the floater and from its back unstrapped the hamper of lunch to get at his fishing tackle. He set the hamper to one side on the grassy bank from which the clump of birches grew.

Something scrabbled in the dam of twisted tree trunks that lay across the stream. At the sound, Blake spun about. A pair of beady eyes stared out at him from beneath a log.

A mink, he thought. Or perhaps an otter. Peering out at him from its den inside the log jam.

"Hello, there," said Blake. "Do you mind if I try my luck."

"Hello, there," said the otter-mink, in a high and piping voice. "What is this luck that you wish to try? Please elucidate."

"What was that you . . ." Blake's voice ran down to a stop.

The otter-mink emerged from beneath the log. It was neither an otter nor a mink. It was a bipedal being—like something that had stepped from the pages of a children's book. A hairy rodent snout was topped by a high domed skull from which flared a pair of pointed ears with tassels on the tips of them. It stood two feet high or so and its body was covered with a smooth, brown coat of fur. It wore a pair of bright red trousers that were mostly pockets and its hands were equipped with long and slender fingers.

Its snout twitched. "Would you, perhaps," it asked in its squeaking voice, "have food inside that basket?"

"Why, yes," said Blake. "I take it you are hungry."

It was absurd, of course. In just a little while—in another minute, if not less—this illustration from a children's book would simply go away and he could get on with his fishing.

"I'm starving," said the illustration. "The people who usually set out food for me have gone on a vacation. I've been scrounging ever since. Have you, perhaps, sometime in your life, tried scrounging for your food?"

"I don't think," said Blake, "that I ever have."

It did not disappear. It kept on staying and it kept on talking and there was no getting rid of it.

Good God, thought Blake, here I go again!

"If you are hungry," he said, "we should get at the hamper. Is there anything, especially, that you like to eat?"

"I eat," said the creature, "anything that *Homo sapiens* can. I am not fussy in the least. My metabolism seems to match most admirably with the denizens of Earth."

Together they walked over to the hamper and Blake lifted off the cover.

"You seem unconcerned," said the creature, "by my appearance from the log jam."

"It's no concern of mine," said Blake, trying to think fast, but unable to prod his mind out of its jog. "We have sandwiches here and some cake and a bowl of, I believe—yes, a bowl of potato salad, and some deviled eggs."

"If you don't mind, I will take a couple of those sandwiches."

"Go right ahead," invited Blake.

"You do not intend to join me?"

"I had breakfast just a while ago."

The creature sat down with a sandwich in each hand and began eating ravenously.

"You must pardon my poor table manners," it said to Blake, "but I have not had any decent food for almost two weeks. I suppose that I expect too much. These people that take care of me set out real food for me. Not like a lot of people do—just a bowl of milk."

Crumbs clung to its trembling whiskers and it went on eating. It finished the two sandwiches and reached out a hand, halted with it poised above the hamper.

"You do not mind?" it asked.

"Not at all," said Blake.

It took another sandwich.

"You will pardon me," it asked, "but how many of you are there?"

"How many of me?"

"Yes, of you. How many of you are there?"

"Why," said Blake, "there is only one of me. How could there be more?"

"It was foolish of me, of course," said the creature, "but when I first saw you, I could have sworn there were more than one of you."

He began eating the sandwich, but at a somewhat slower rate than he'd employed on the other two.

He finished it and dabbed delicately at his whiskers, knocking off the crumbs.

"I thank you very much," he said.

"You are most welcome," said Blake. "Are you sure you won't have another one?"

"Not a sandwich, perhaps. But if you had some cake to spare."

"Help yourself," said Blake.

The creature helped itself.

"And now," said Blake, "you've asked me a question. Would you say it might be fair if I asked you one."

"Very fair, indeed," the creature said. "Go ahead and ask it."

"I have found myself wondering," said Blake, "exactly who and what you are."

"Why bless you," said the creature, "I thought that you would know. It never occurred to me that you wouldn't recognize me."

Blake shook his head. "I'm sorry, but I don't."

"I am a Brownie," said the creature, bowing. "At your service, sir."

9

Dr. Michael Daniels was waiting at his desk when Blake was ushered into his office.

"How are you feeling this morning?" Daniels asked.

Blake grinned bleakly. "Not too badly, after the going over you gave me yesterday. Were there any tests that you left out?"

"We sort of threw the book at you," Daniels admitted. "There's still a test or two, if . . ."

"No, thank you."

Daniels gestured at a chair. "Make yourself comfortable. We have some things to talk about."

Blake took the indicated chair. Daniels pulled a fat folder in front of him and opened it.

"I would assume," said Blake, "that you have been doing some checking on what might have happened out in space—what happened to me, I mean. Any luck at all?"

Daniels shook his head. "None. We've gone over the passenger and crew lists of all missing ships. That is, Space Administration has. They're as interested in this as I am, perhaps even more so."

"Passenger lists wouldn't tell you much," said Blake. "I'd be just a name and we don't know . . ."

"True," said Daniels, "but there are also fingerprints and voice prints. And you aren't there."

"Somehow I got out into space. . . ."

"Yes, we know you did. Also someone froze you.

Someone took the trouble to freeze you. If we could find out why someone did that, we'd know a lot more than we do. But, of course, when a ship is lost, the records are lost."

"I've been doing some thinking myself," said Blake. "We have been presuming all the time that I was frozen so that my life would be spared. Which means it was done before whatever happened to the ship had come about. How could anyone know what was going to happen? Oh, I suppose there would be situations where they would. Have you ever thought that I was frozen and thrown off the ship because they didn't want me aboard, because I'd done something or they were afraid of me or something of the sort?"

"No," said Daniels, "I had never thought of that. I had thought, however, that you may not have been the only one frozen and encapsulated, that it might have been done to others and that they still are out there. You just happened to be the one that was found. Given time, it could be a way in which a long shot could be taken to save some lives—I would suspect important lives."

"Let's get back to this business of them giving me the old heave-ho off the ship. If I had been such a louse that they felt they had to pitchfork me into space, why the elaborate attempt to save my life?"

Daniels shook his head. "I couldn't even guess. All we're doing is dealing in assumptions. You may have to resign yourself to the possibility that you will never know. I had hoped that you would be able to dig back to a re-cognition of your past, but you haven't so far. There's a fairly good chance you may never be able to. After a while we can resort to some psychiatric treatment that could help. Although I'll tell you quite frankly that it may not."

"Are you telling me to give up?"

"No. Just trying to tell you the truth. We'll keep on

trying so long as you're willing to go along with us. But I thought we owed it to you to tell you there is a chance we'll never get an answer."

"That's fair enough," said Blake.

"How did the fishing go the other day?" asked Daniels.

"All right," said Blake. "I caught six trout and had a good day in the open. Which, I suspect, was what you wanted."

"Any hallucinations?"

"Yes," said Blake. "There was a hallucination. I didn't tell you about it. Just held it back. Decided this morning I'd tell you. What's one hallucination more or less? When I was out fishing I met a Brownie."

"Oh," said Daniels.

"Didn't you hear what I said I met a Brownie. I talked with him. He ate up most of my lunch. You know what I mean. One of those little folks that appear in children's stories. With big pointed ears and a high, peaked cap. Only this one didn't have a cap. And he had a rodent face."

"You were fortunate. It's not many people who ever see a Brownie. Fewer yet who talk with them."

"You mean there are such things!"

"Why, yes, of course there are. A migrant people from the Coonskin stars. Not very many of them. The root stock was brought to earth . . . oh, I'd guess a hundred, a hundred and fifty years ago. One of the exploration ships. The idea was that the Brownies would visit us for a short while—a sort of cultural exchange, I gather—then would go back home. But they liked it here and formally applied for permission to stay. After that they scattered, disappeared gradually. They took to the woods. There they found places to live—burrows, caves, hollow trees."

He shook his head in some perplexity.

"A strange people. They rejected most of the material advantages that we offered them. Wanted nothing to do with our civilization, were unimpressed with our culture, but they liked the planet. Liked it as a place to live, but in their own way, of course. We don't know too much about them. Highly civilized, it would appear, but in a different way than we. Intelligent, but with different values from the ones we hold. Some of them, I understand, have attached themselves to certain families or individuals who set out food for them, or supply them cloth for clothing, or other needs they may have from time to time. It is a curious relationship. The Brownies aren't pets of these people. Maybe you could call them good luck talismen. Much the relationship that the literary Brownies were assigned."

"Well, I'll be damned," said Blake.

"You thought your Brownie was another hallucination?"

"Yes, I did. I expected him to go away all the time, to simply vanish from my sight. But he didn't. He sat there eating and wiping the crumbs off his whiskers and telling me where to place the flies. Over there, he'd say, there's a big one over there just between that swirl of water and the bank. And there would be. He seemed to know where the fish were."

"He was paying you back for the lunch. He was giving you good luck."

"You think he actually did know where the fish were? I know, it seemed to me he did, but . . ."

"I wouldn't be surprised," said Daniels. "As I told you, we don't know too much about the Brownies. They probably have abilities we lack. Knowing where to find the fish might be one of them." He glanced sharply at Blake. "You'd never heard about the Brownies? The real ones, I mean."

"No, I never had."

"I think that gives us a good time peg," said Daniels.

"If you had been here, on Earth, at that time, you would have heard about it."

"Maybe I did, but don't remember."

"I don't think so. The incident, to judge from the writings at the time, made a great public impression. It's something that you would have recalled if you'd ever heard of it. It would have made a deep impression on your mind."

"We have other time pegs," said Blake. "This get-up that we wear is new to me. Robes and shorts and sandals. I can recall that I wore some sort of trousers and a jerkin. And the ships. The gravity grids are new to me. I can remember that we used nuclear power. . . ."

"We still do."

"Nuclear power alone in my day. Now it is an auxiliary force to build up greater velocity, but the real power comes from the control and manipulation of gravitational forces."

"There are a number of other things that are new to you, too," said Daniels. "The houses . . ."

"They almost drove me crazy to start with," Blake said. "But I'm relieved about that Brownie. It subtracts one potential incident from my situation."

"These hallucinations. You don't think they are, of course. You told me yesterday."

"I can't see how they can be," said Blake. "I remember everything that happens up to a certain point, then there is a blank and finally I'm myself again. I can't remember a thing that happened during that blank period, although there is abundant evidence that something did transpire. And there is a definite period of time to account for it."

"The second one," said Daniels, "happened while you slept."

"True. But the Room observed a certain phenomena, which transpired over a definite period of time."

"What kind of house do you have?"

"A Norman-Gilson B258."

"One of the newer and better models," Daniels told him. "Beautifully instrumented and computerized. Practically foolproof. Not much that could go wrong with one of them."

"I don't think anything did go wrong," said Blake. "I think the Room told the truth. I think something was happening in that room. When I woke up I was on the floor . . ."

"But with no idea of what had happened, not until the Room told you. No idea as to why these things happen?"

"None at all. I had hoped you might have some idea."

"Not, actually," said Daniels. "No real idea, that is. There are two things about you—how do I say this?—well, that are confusing. Your physical condition, for one thing. You look like a man of thirty, perhaps the middle thirties. There are some lines in your face. You have the appearance of maturity. And yet your body is the body of a youth. There is no breakdown, no sign that breakdown is beginning. You're a perfect physical specimen. And if you're that, why the facial appearance of thirty?"

"And the other thing? You said there were two."

"The other? Well, your electro-encephalogram shows up a strange pattern. The main brain pattern is there and recognizable. But there is something else as well. Almost—and I hesitate to say this—but almost as if another, or other brain patterns were transposed on your own. Rather feeble brain patterns, subsidiary patterns probably would be the way to say it, showing up, but not too strongly."

"What are you trying to say, doctor? That there is something wrong mentally? Which would explain the hallucinations, of course. Which might mean there really are hallucinations."

Daniels shook his head. "No, not that. But strange. Nothing to indicate any malfunction. Nothing that would indicate any brain deterioration. Your mind, apparently, is as healthy and as normal as your body. But almost as if you had more than one brain. Although we know, of course, that you have only one. The X-rays show that very clearly."

"You're sure that I am human?"

"Your body says you are. Why do you ask?"

"I don't know," said Blake. "You found me out in space. I came from space . . ."

"I see," said Daniels. "But forget about it. There is no shred of evidence that you're anything but human. The overwhelming evidence is that you are."

"And now what? I go back home and wait for more of these . . ."

"Not right away," said Daniels. "We'd like you to stay with us for awhile. A few more days. If you are willing."

"More tests?"

"Well, perhaps. I'd like to talk with some of my colleagues, let some of them look at you. They may have something to offer. Mostly, I guess I'd like you to stay for some further observation."

"In case there is another hallucination?"

"Something like that," said Daniels.

"This brain business bothers me," said Blake. "More than one, you say . . ."

"No. Just a suggestion of the encephalogram. I wouldn't worry about it."

"O.K.," said Blake, "I won't."

But what was it that Brownie had asked? How many of you are there? I could have sworn, when I first looked at you, that there was more than one of you.

"Doctor, about this Brownie . . ."

"What about the Brownie?"

"Nothing, I guess," said Blake. "Nothing that's important."

10

Excerpt from proceedings of senatorial inquiry (regional, Washington, North America) into the proposal for a program of biological engineering as the basis for a colonizing policy on other solar systems.

MR. PETER DOTY, committee counsel: Your name is Austin Lukas?

DR. LUKAS: Yes, sir. I reside in Tenafly, New Jersey and am employed at Biologics, Inc., in New York City—Manhattan.

MR. DOTY: You head up the research department of that company, do you not?

DR. LUKAS: I am the chief of one of the research programs.

MR. DOTY: And this program deals with bioengineering?

DR. LUKAS: Yes sir, it does. At the moment we are especially concerned with the problem of developing an all-purpose agricultural animal.

MR. DOTY: Would you please explain.

DR. LUKAS: Gladly. Our hope is to be able to develop an animal which will provide several different types of meat, that will give milk, provide wool or hair or fur, perhaps all three. It would replace, we would hope, the many specialized animals which man has used in his animal husbandry since the Neolithic Revolution.

SENATOR STONE: And I take it, Dr. Lukas, that you

have some indications your research may result in some practical success.

DR. LUKAS: Indeed we do. I might say that we have the basic problems licked. We actually have a herd of these animals. What we are trying for now are certain refinements. We have as our goal the development of a single animal which will replace all the other farm animals, supplying everything they now supply.

SENATOR STONE: And in this you also have some hope of success?

DR. LUKAS: We are very much encouraged.

SENATOR STONE: And what do you call this animal that you have now, may I ask?

DR. LUKAS: We have no name for it, senator. We haven't even bothered to try to think of one.

SENATOR STONE: It wouldn't be a cow, would it?

DR. LUKAS: No, not entirely. It would have some bovine aspects, naturally.

SENATOR STONE: Nor a pig? Nor sheep?

DR. LUKAS: No, neither of those. Not entirely, of course. But with some characteristics of both.

SENATOR HORTON: I think that there is no need to go through these long preliminaries. What my distinguished colleague wants to ask you is whether this creature you are developing is something entirely new in the way of life—a synthetic life, let's say—or whether it still can claim some relationship to present and natural forms?

DR. LUKAS: That, senator, is an extremely difficult question to answer. One could say, in all truthfulness, that the present and natural forms of life have been retained and used as patterns, but that what we have is essentially a new kind of animal.

SENATOR STONE: Thank you, sir. And I wish also to thank my fellow senator for his quick preception of the direction in which my questioning was leading. So here we have, you would say, an entirely new kind of creature, distantly associated, perhaps, with a cow, a pig, a sheep, perhaps with even other forms of life . . .

DR. LUKAS: Yes, with other forms of life. There may be a limit somewhere, of course, but at the moment we do not see it. We feel we may be able to keep on drafting various forms of life, fusing them together into something viable . . .

SENATOR STONE: And the further you go in this direction, the further you take this life form from its association with any present form of life?

DR. LUKAS: Yes, I suppose you could say that. I'd have to think about it before I gave an answer.

SENATOR STONE: Now, doctor, let me inquire into the state of the art. You can do this biological engineering with animals. Could the same thing be done with human beings?

DR. LUKAS: Oh, yes. Certainly it could.

SENATOR STONE: You feel certain that new types of humanity could be created in the laboratory. Perhaps many different types.

DR. LUKAS: I have no doubt of it.

SENATOR STONE: And once this had been done— once you had engineered a human to specific specifications, would that human breed true to the form you had created?

DR. LUKAS: There is no question of that. The animals we have created have bred true. It should be no different with a human. It is simply a matter of altering the genetic material. That is what must be done in the first place, you understand.

SENATOR STONE: Let us get this straight now. Suppose you did develop a new human strain, then that strain would reproduce other humans of the self-same strain?

DR. LUKAS: Exactly. Except, of course, for the tiny

mutations and the variations which are implicit in the evolutionary processes. But that occurs even in the natural forms. That is how all life today evolved.

SENATOR STONE: And say you did create a new type of human being. Say, for example, one that would be able to exist under a condition of much higher gravity than we have here on earth, one that could breathe a different kind of air, one that could thrive on food which might be poisonous to the human being as he now exists, would you . . . Let me rephrase that question, if you don't mind. Would it be possible, would you say, to engineer such a life form?

DR. LUKAS: You're asking only for my considered opinion, of course.

SENATOR STONE: That is right.

DR. LUKAS: Well, then, I'd say it would be entirely possible. First, you would have to take into consideration all the factors involved and then draft the biological blueprint and . . .

SENATOR STONE: But it could be done?

DR. LUKAS: Without any doubt at all.

SENATOR STONE: You could design a being which could exist under almost any planetary condition?

DR. LUKAS: Senator, I must make it clear that I couldn't. The bioengineering of humans would not fall into my particular field. But yes, it does lie within the state of the art to do this. There are men working with the problem today who could do it. Not that there is any serious attempt at the moment to actually create such a human, but the problems, I understand, have been worked out.

SENATOR STONE: And the procedures, also?

DR. LUKAS: That is my understanding. The procedures also.

SENATOR STONE: And these men, working with these

procedures, could design and create a human which would be able to live under any planetary condition?

DR. LUKAS: Well, not quite that sweeping, senator. Not any condition. Eventually perhaps, but not now. And there would, of course, be certain conditions which would be entirely incompatible with life of any sort.

SENATOR STONE: But a form of human life could be created which would exist under a number of conditions which at the moment would prohibit human life as we know it.

DR. LUKAS: I think that can stand as a fair statement.

SENATOR STONE: Then let me ask you, doctor . . . if such a life form were created, would it still be human?

DR. LUKAS: It would be based, so far as possible, upon the biological and intellectual pattern of a human being. This would be necessary. You have to have a starting point.

SENATOR STONE: Would it look like a human being?

DR. LUKAS: In many cases, it would not.

SENATOR STONE: In most cases, perhaps. Wouldn't that be right, doctor?

DR. LUKAS: It would depend entirely upon the severity of the environmental parameters which would have to be met.

SENATOR STONE: In some cases, it would be a monster, would it not?

DR. LUKAS: Senator, you will have to define your terms. What is a monster?

SENATOR STONE: All right, then. Let us say a monster is a life form that would be repugnant for a human being to look upon. A life form in which a human being could see no relationship to himself. A life form, confronted with which, a human might find himself terrified or horrified or filled with loathing and disgust.

DR. LUKAS: Whether a man would be filled with loathing and disgust would depend, to a large extent, upon what kind of man he was. With the proper attitude . . .

SENATOR STONE: Let us forget about the proper attitude. Let us take an ordinary man or woman, any one of the people sitting in this room. Might certain people look upon this hypothetical creation of yours and feel loathing and disgust?

DR. LUKAS: I suppose some of them would. And I want to correct you, senator. You say monster. This is not my monster. It is something you have conjured up. . . .

SENATOR STONE: But some human beings would regard such a creature as a monster?

DR. LUKAS: Some of them.

SENATOR STONE: Many of them, perhaps.

DR. LUKAS: Yes. Perhaps many of them.

SENATOR STONE: Thank you, doctor. I believe that is all the questions that I have.

SENATOR HORTON: Now, Dr. Lukas, let's take a little further look at this synthetic man. I know that description is not entirely right, but I think it may please my colleague.

SENATOR STONE: A synthetic man, yes. Not a human being. What this so-called bioengineering proposal calls for is to colonize other planets, not with human beings, but with synthetic creatures which would bear no resemblance to human beings. In other words, to release upon the galaxy, a horde of monsters.

SENATOR HORTON: Well, now, let's see. Dr. Lukas, let you and me agree with Senator Stone that such a creature might be fairly horrible to look upon. But how it might look would seem to me to be beside the question. What is important is what it is. Do you agree?

DR. LUKAS: Most emphatically, sir.

SENATOR HORTON: Aside from how it might look, would you say it still would be a human being?

DR. LUKAS: Yes, senator, I would. Its bodily structure would bear no relationship to what it would be. Its identity would rest within its brain and mind, its motivations and its intellectual outlook.

SENATOR HORTON: And its brain would be a human brain?

DR. LUKAS: Yes, sir.

SENATOR HORTON: Therefore its emotions and motivations and outlook would conform to the human framework?

DR. LUKAS: Certainly they would.

SENATOR HORTON: Therefore, it would be human. No matter what its form, it still would be human.

DR. LUKAS: Yes, human.

SENATOR HORTON: Doctor, to your knowledge, has such a creature ever been made? By creature, I mean, of course, a synthetic human.

DR. LUKAS: Yes. A matter of two hundred years ago or so. Two of them were made. But there was a difference . . .

SENATOR STONE: Just a minute, there! Are you referring to that old myth we hear occasionally. . . .

DR. LUKAS: Senator, it is not a myth.

SENATOR STONE: Have you documentation to back up your statement?

DR. LUKAS: No, sir.

SENATOR STONE: What do you mean—no, sir? How can you come before this hearing and make a statement that you can't back up?

SENATOR HORTON: I can back it up. At the proper time I shall place the necessary documents in evidence.

SENATOR STONE: Perhaps, then, the senator should be sitting where the witness is . . .

SENATOR HORTON: Not at all. I'm perfectly satisfied with this witness. You say, sir, that there was a difference . . .

SENATOR STONE: Just a moment, there! I object! I do not think this witness is competent.

SENATOR HORTON: Well, let's find out. Dr. Lukas, under what circumstances did you come upon this information?

DR. LUKAS: About ten years ago, when I was doing some research for a paper, I applied for clearance to have access to certain records in Space Administration. You see, senator, I was following up what you call a myth. Not many people knew of it, but I had heard of it and wondered if it might not be more than a myth. So I applied for clearance. . . .

SENATOR HORTON: And you were given clearance?

DR. LUKAS: Well, not right away, Space Administration was—well, you might call it reluctant. So finally I took the tack that in a matter a good two centuries old, no clearance was needed. That it no longer was a matter of clearance, but a matter of historical record. I don't mind telling you that I had a rough time making anyone see the logic of my argument.

SENATOR HORTON: But you finally prevailed?

DR. LUKAS: Yes, finally. With considerable competent assistance, I might add. You see, the records at one time had been under the highest top security such material could be given. Technically, this security still applied. It took considerable argument to make it apparent that such a situation was ridiculous . . .

SENATOR STONE: Now, hold up a minute, doctor. Before you go on, one question. You said you had assistance.

DR. LUKAS: Yes, I did.

SENATOR STONE: Could a considerable part of that assistance have come from Senator Horton?

SENATOR HORTON: Since the question concerns me, I'll answer if Dr. Lukas will consent. I am quite happy to admit that I did lend him some assistance.

SENATOR STONE: All right, that's all I wanted. Just so it's on the record.

SENATOR HORTON: Dr. Lukas, if you'll please continue.

DR. LUKAS: The records showed that two hundred and twenty one years ago—2266, to be exact—two synthetic beings had been made. They were in the shape of humans and they had human minds, but they were constructed for a very special purpose. They were to be used in intial contacts with life on other planets, to be carried aboard exploratory and survey ships and used to gather data on the dominant life on whatever new planets might be found.

SENATOR HORTON: Now, Dr. Lukas, without going into details at the present moment, can you tell us exactly how it was planned they were to do this sort of job?

DR. LUKAS: I'm not sure I can make myself entirely clear, but I'll try. These synthetic humans were highly adaptable. You might have described them, for want of a better term, as plastic. The concept of open-endedness was employed—it couldn't have been developed earlier than ten years or so before, and it is unusual, to say the least, to find a concept as intricate as this bent to practical purpose in such a length of time. All the basic components of the constructed human bodies involved open-endedness—completed, you understand, and yet, in a sense, essentially incomplete. The amino acids . . .

SENATOR HORTON: Perhaps, for the moment, you will only tell us what these bodies were intended to do, without going into the principles involved.

DR. LUKAS: You mean simply how they were intended to function?

SENATOR HORTON: If you will, please.

DR. LUKAS: The idea was that once an exploratory ship

landed on a planet one of the dominant species of that planet would be captured and be scanned. You are familiar, I think, with the biological scanning process. The structure, the chemistry, the metabolic processes—all the data which made the creature what it was—would be determined. This data would be stored in a memory core. Once this was done, the data would be transmitted to the simulated human which, because of the uniqueness of its biological open-endedness, would change into an exact copy of the creature which was described by the data in the tapes. This would not have been a slow process. Any delay would have been fatal. It must have been an uncanny thing to watch—a human being almost instantaneously changing into an alien creature.

SENATOR HORTON: You say the human would have changed into the alien creature. Does that mean in every respect—mental, intellectual, if the term implies, as well as . . .

DR. LUKAS: The human would, in fact, become the creature. Not one of the creatures, you understand, but an exact copy of the creature from which it had been patterned. It would have that creature's memories and its mind. It would be able to pick up immediately where the other creature had left off. Released from the ship, it could seek out that creature's fellows and rejoin them and could carry out its investigations . . .

SENATOR HORTON: You mean it still would retain the human mind as well?

DR. LUKAS: Well, that would be hard to say. The human mentality and memory and identity and all the rest of it would still be there, although perhaps deeply sublimated. It would exist as a subconscious that could be triggered to the surface. A compulsion would be planted for the human-turned-creature to return to the ship after a stated interval of time and once returned, it would be induced to revert to its human form. Once back in human form, it would be able to recall the memories of its existence as an alien creature and data which otherwise might have been impossible to obtain would be made available.

SENATOR HORTON: And, may I ask, how did this all work out?

DR. LUKAS: That, sir, is hard to say. There are no reports as to results. There are records of them—both of them—having been sent out. But after that there is only silence.

SENATOR HORTON: Your surmise would be that something went wrong?

DR. LUKAS: Yes. But I can't imagine what it might have been.

SENATOR HORTON: Something to do with the simulated men, perhaps.

DR. LUKAS: Yes, that could be the case. There is no way of knowing.

SENATOR HORTON: They didn't work, perhaps.

DR. LUKAS: Oh, they would have performed their function. There could have been no reason for them not to perform as they were planned. They would have had to work.

SENATOR HORTON: I ask these questions because I know that if I do not, my distinguished colleague will. Now let me ask you one of my own. Could such a simulated man be constructed today?

DR. LUKAS: Yes, with the blueprints in our hands, there would be not a bit of trouble to build another one.

SENATOR HORTON: But no others were ever built, so far as you know, that is.

DR. LUKAS: So far as I know.

SENATOR HORTON: Would you care to speculate . . .

DR. LUKAS: No, senator, I would not.

SENATOR STONE: If I may interrupt. Dr. Lukas, do you have some sort of descriptive term for the process which was employed to make such men as these?

DR. LUKAS: Yes, as a matter of fact, we have. It is called the werewolf principle.

11

In the parking lot across the street a man carried a tub out of the back door of one of the houses and set it on the patio at the edge of the pool. A tree was planted in the tub and when the man had set it down and moved away the tree began to ring—emitting a sound like the happy ringing of many silver bells.

Blake, sitting on a chair and wrapped in a robe of candy-colored stripes, leaned his elbows on the railing five stories above the street, and strained his ears, trying to make certain that the ringing really came from the tree. It seemed incredible, but there had been no such silver sound until the tub in which the tree was planted had been set beside the pool. And his ears told him that the sound did, indeed, come from the direction of the house.

Washington dozed in the blue smokiness of a late October afternoon. A few ground cars went past on the boulevard below, their air jet making soft, sighing sounds as they moved along. In the far distance, over the Potomac, a few floaters bobbed along—floating chairs with humans sitting in them. The houses in the parking lot were lined up in orderly rows, each with its bright green lawn, its beds of brightly colored autumn flowers, the blue shine of the pools. By leaning forward and craning his neck, he could just make out his own house, down the boulevard, third row from the front, squatting on the foundation where it had put down.

His nearest neighbor on the solarium porch was an elderly man, muffled to the ears in a thick red blanket, blank eyes staring out into the space beyond the railing, seeing nothing, mumbling to himself. A short distance away two patients were playing a game that might have been checkers.

An attendant came hurrying across the porch.

"Mr. Blake," he said, "there is someone here to see you."

Blake rose and turned around. Standing in the door that led out onto the porch was a woman, tall, dark-haired, wearing a robe of pale rose, a material that had the sheen of silk.

"Miss Horton," said Blake. "Yes, please show her in."

She came across the porch and held out her hand to him.

"I drove down to your village yesterday afternoon," she said, "and found that you had left."

"I am sorry," said Blake, "that I was not there. Won't you please sit down."

She seated herself in a chair and Blake perched on the railing.

"You and your father are in Washington," he said. "The hearings . . ."

She nodded. "They began this morning."

"You'll be attending some of them, I suppose."

"I suppose," she said. "But it's a painful thing. It's hard to see my father take the beating he will take. I admire him, of course, for standing on the thing that he believes, but I could wish that, occasionally, he might plop for something that carried public approval. But he almost never does. He's always on the wrong side, so far as the public is concerned. And this one is the one that can really hurt him."

"You mean this business of unanimity. I was reading something about it just the other day. It seems to me a foolish setup."

"Perhaps it is," she said, "but that's the way it is. It is carrying the rule of the majority to unnecessary limits. It will half kill the senator if he has to retire from public life. It has been meat and bread to him for all the years he's lived."

"I liked your father very much," said Blake. "There's something natural about him, something that corresponds to the house you live in."

"You mean old-fashioned."

"Well, maybe. Although that's not it exactly. There is something solid about the man, and yet he has an enthusiasm and an apparent dedication. . . ."

"Oh, yes," she said. "He has dedication. And you must admire him for it and I think that mostly people do. But he manages somehow or other to irritate a lot of people by showing them they're wrong."

Blake laughed. "I don't know of a better way to irritate the people."

"Perhaps," she said. "But how about yourself?"

"I'm getting along quite well," he said. "There really is no reason why I should be here. Before you came I was sitting here, listening to a tree ring a lot of bells. I couldn't quite believe my senses. A man across the street brought one out of the house and set it by a pool and it began to ring."

She leaned forward to stare across the street. The tree emitted a rippling peal of bonging bells.

"A monastery tree," she said. "There are not too many of them. A few of them are imported from a planet—one quite far out, I can't recall which one."

"Continually," said Blake, "I'm running up against these things that are entirely new to me. Things that are outside my entire circle of experience. Just the other day I met a Brownie."

She stared at him, delighted. "A Brownie! You mean you really did?"

He nodded. "It ate all my lunch," he said.

"Oh, how nice for you! Most people never see one."

"I'd never heard of them," he said. "I thought that I was having another hallucination."

"Like the time you came to our house."

"That's right. I still don't know what happened that night. There is no explaining it."

"The doctors . . ."

"The doctors don't seem to be much help. They are as puzzled as I am. I think, perhaps, the Brownie might have come the closest to a guess."

"The Brownie? What would he have to do with it?"

"He asked me how many there were of me. He said he felt quite sure, when he first saw me, that there was more than one of me. Two men in one, three men in one . . . I wouldn't know how many. More than one, he said."

"Mr. Blake," she said, "I think that every man is more than just one man. He has many sides to him."

He shook his head. "That's not what the Brownie meant. I am sure it wasn't. I've been doing a lot of thinking about it and I'm sure he wasn't talking about different temperaments."

"You've told this to your doctor?"

"Well, no, I guess I haven't. The poor guy has enough to worry him. This would be just another thing."

"But important, maybe."

"I wouldn't know," said Blake.

"You act," said Elaine Horton, "almost as if you didn't care, as if you didn't want to find out what has happened to you. Or, perhaps, that you are afraid to find out."

He glanced sharply at her. "I hadn't thought of it quite that way," he said, "but you may well be right."

Across the way the bell-sounds changed—no longer the trilling of many silver bells, but the sonorous clanging of a bell much larger, calling out a warning and a challenge across the rooftops of the ancient city.

12

Fear thundered in the tunnel. There was the reek of alien odors and an alien muttering. Light bounced off the walls and the floor was hard as rock.

The creature crouched and whimpered, every muscle tensed, each separate nerve frayed with paralyzing fear.

The tunnel went on endlessly and there was no escape. It was caught and trapped. And it had no idea where it might be trapped. Certainly in a place such as it had never known before and a place it had not sought. It had been caught and dumped here and for no reason that it knew.

There had been a time before and then it had been wet and hot and dark, with the creepy feeling of many tiny life forms. And now it was hot and bright and dry, but there was no sense of tiny life forms—rather the sense of distant larger life forms and the thunder of their thoughts that rumbled like a drum within the brain.

The creature wheeled about, half rising from its crouch, toenails clicking on the hardness of the floor. The tunnel still went on, in back as well as front. An enclosed place where there were not any stars. But there was the talk—the thought-talk and the deeper rumble of the spoken talk—not the kind of talk that trickled from the stars, but jumbled and chaotic talk, a murky talk that surged and flared and hadn't any depth and not a shred of meaning.

A tunnel world, the creature thought in terror, a narrow, enclosed space that went on and on forever, reeking with its odors and filled with murky talk and awash with fear.

There were openings, it saw, all along the tunnel, and some of them were closed with a dark material, while there were others open, leading, more than likely, into other tunnels that went on and on, as endlessly as this.

Far down the tunnel a creature, huge, misshapen, terrible, came from one of the openings. It made a clicking sound as it walked and it turned toward the creature, coming down the tunnel. It screamed and something that it carried clattered on the floor and the sound of its wrenching terror, welling from its brain, bounced back and forth like shrieks along the tunnel walls. It turned and ran, moving very rapidly, the vocalization of its fear combining with the bouncing reverberations of the terror that welled within its brain to fill the tunnel to bursting with the turmoil of the sound.

The creature moved, its toenails scratching desperately on the hard material, its body flashing toward the nearest opening that led outward from the tunnel. Inside its body its viscera curled and tightened with the panic that surged through it and its brain grew dim and limp with fear and it felt the darkness coming down upon it like a great weight which dropped from some great height. And suddenly it was not itself, it was not within the tunnel, it was back again in that place of warm, black comfort which had been its prison.

Blake skidded to a halt beside his bed and in the moment of his skidding, wondered why he ran and why his hospital gown should be lying on the floor and he naked in the room. And in that second of his wonder there was a snapping in his skull as if something inside his head, too tightly bound, had ripped, and he knew about the tunnel and the fear and those other two who were one with him.

He dropped down to sit upon the bed and happiness

gushed through him. He was whole again: he was the creature he had been before. Now he no longer was alone, but with the other two.—Hiyah, pals, he whispered and they answered back, not with words, but with a huddling of their minds.

(Clasped hands and brotherhood. Sharp, cold stars above a desert of drifted sand and snow. The reaching out and snaring of the data from the stars. The hot and steaming swamp. The long weighing of the data inside the pyramid that was a biological computer. The swift, mutual pooling of three separate pools of thought. The touch of minds, one against another.)

—It ran when it saw me, Quester said. There'll be others coming.

—This is your planet, Changer. You know what to do.

—Yes, Thinker, Changer said, my planet. But our knowledge is one knowledge.

—But you're the quicker at it. The knowledge is too much, there is too much of it. We follow you, but slowly.

—Thinker's right, said Quester. The decision's up to you.

—They may not know it's me, said Changer. Not right away. We may have a little time.

—But not too much.

—No, Quester, not too much.

And that was right, thought Blake. There would be little time. The screaming nurse racing down the hall would bring the others tumbling out—internes, other nurses, doctors, the maintenance men and the people in the kitchen. In just a few more minutes the hospital would become a churning turmoil.

—The trouble is, he said, that Quester looks too much like a wolf.

—Your definition, Quester said, means one that eats another. You know that I would never . . .

No, Blake told himself. No, of course you wouldn't, Quester. But they will think you would. When they see you they will think you are a wolf. Like the guard that night at the senator's, seeing you outlined against the lightning flash. And filled with the old folklore of wolves, reacted instinctively.

And if anyone should see Thinker, what would they think of him?—What happened to us, Changer? Quester asked. Twice I broke free, once in wet and dark, again in light and narrow.

—Once I broke free, said Thinker, and I could not function.

—Later we will think of that, said Changer. Now we're in a jam. We must get out of here.

—Changer, Quester said, we must stay as you. If, later, we need running, I can run.

—And I, said Thinker, if we need it later—I can be anything at all.

"Quiet," said Blake aloud. "Quiet. Let me think a second."

13

First, there had been himself, a human—a simulated human, an android, a man made in a laboratory, the open-endedness, the werewolf principle, the biological and intellectual flexibility which shaped him as he was.

A man. A man in everything but breeding. And a better man than a normal man could ever be. Immune to illnesses, self-healing, self-repairing. With the same intellect, the same emotion, the same physiological processes as any other man. But a tool as well, an instrument—a man designed to do a certain job. An infiltrator of the alien form. An so psychologically balanced, so unhumanly logical, so flexible, so perceptive that he could change into an alien form and assume an alien intellect and alien emotion without the mental violence that might tear a normal man apart.

Second, there had been the Thinker (what else could one call it?)—a formless mass of flesh that could assume any shape it wished, but which through long convention preferred a pyramidal shape as the optimum for function. A dweller in the raw savagery of a swampland planet—a primal place where a new-born sun poured out a withering flood of light and energy. Monstrous forms crawled and swam and shambled through the swamps, but the Thinkers had no fear of them or any need of fear. Drawing their very sustenance from the overpowering storm of energy that lashed the planet, they had their own unique defense, an envelope of interlocking lines of force which walled them in against the ravening world they inhabited. There was, for them, no thought of life or death, but only of existence—for there was no record nor remembrance of birth, no instance where one had ever died. Brute physical forces, under certain circumstances, could dismember them, scattering the flesh, but from each piece of sundered flesh, packed with the genetic memory of the entire creature, a new entity would arise. Not that this had ever happened, but the knowledge that it could happen and its consequences was a part of the basic mental information with which each Thinker was equipped.

The Changer and the Thinker, and the Changer had become the Thinker—by the wiles and schemes and the tricky techniques of that other tribe of thinkers many light-years distance, a simulated man became another creature, with all that creature's thoughts and memories, with all its attitudes and motives, with all its physiological and psychological equipment. Became, in effect, the other creature, but still with enough of man left in him that he recoiled and cringed away from the terror and the solemn greatness of the thing he had become, saved only by the mental armor that had been built into him on that planet so far off that, from this point in space, its sun could not be seen.

Cringed away, but only marginally—only in the hidden corners of the mind stuff that was the alien creature. For he was the creature and the human part of him was driven deep into the folds of solid flesh and mystic mind that made the creature of the swamps. But as time went on the human mind emerged to take its rightful place, the horror now submerged and finally forgotten, having learned to live in this new body on this different world, enraptured and thrilled and filled with bursting wonder at this new experience of two minds existing side by side, neither claiming ascendency of the other, not jockeying for position, not contending, for they both belonged to an entity that now was no longer purely human or purely creature of the swamps, but the two of them in one.

The sun blazed down and the body sucked in the energy and the swamp was a place of beauty because it was the creature's home. A new life was there to touch, to explore and comprehend, to wonder at and appreciate—a new life and a new world and an added viewpoint for both the alien and the mentality of humanity.

There was a favorite Thinking Place and there was the Favorite Thought and at times (not often) a shadowy communication with other fellow creatures, a hazy reaching out of minds that brushed against each other briefly, like a hand-touch in the dark, and then withdrew. For while communication was possible, there was little need of it; each of the Thinkers was sufficient to itself.

Time had no meaning, nor did space, except insomuch as either one or the both of them were considerations in the Thought. For the Thought was all—it was the reason for existence, it was the task and dedication, and it was pointed toward no end, not even the completion of itself, for there could be no end to it. It was a thing that went on endlessly and it fed upon itself and there was no belief nor hope that it ever would be done.

But time now was a factor, for the human mind was triggered to a time when it must return and it had returned and the Thinker became a man again. The data that the man had gathered was packed into a memory core and the ship leaped into space again and went on and on.

Now there was another planet and another creature and the Changer became the other creature as he had become the Thinker and went out upon the planet in the guise of the creature that he had become.

The planet was as cold and dry as the first had been hot and damp, with the feeble sun far off and the stars glittering like sharp, hard diamonds in the cloudless sky, the ground dusted with the white of snow and sand, drifted into dunes by thin and keening winds that swept the land at frequent intervals.

Now the human mind ran in the body of a Quester that ran in a pack of Questers across the frigid plains and along the rocky ridges, running with a pagan joy beneath the diamond stars and the lanterns of the moons, seeking out those holy places where by long tradition they held communion with the stars. But by long tradition only, for at any time or place, they could snare the pictures radioed out unconsciously by the many cultures that lived on other solar systems.

Not understanding the pictures, nor even trying or wishing for an understanding—simply grasping them and holding them for the esthetic value that could be gained from them. Like a human, thought the human mind inside the Quester body, might wander the galleries of an art exhibit, to stop and stare at some painting which held within its color and its composition a truth that spoke in silent tongue—a truth that could not be told in words, but that need not be told in words.

A human mind inside the Quester body, and another mind as well; a mind that came creeping out and a mind that should not be there, that should have disappeared when the simulated human had shed the body in which that mind was housed.

The clever men on earth had not planned it that way, had not dreamed that it would happen that way, had thought that alien mind and body could be gotten rid of and would not occur again, that the simulated human they had fashioned could be wiped clean as a slate is wiped and go on to something else.

But there was no wiping clean, there was no erasure. The memory and the pattern did not go away, could not be scrubbed away. They remained. They might be driven deep into the consciousness of the reawakened human, but they crept out again.

So not two creatures ran the plains of drifted sand and snow, but three, all three occupying the body of the Quester. And while the Quester snared the pictures from the stars, the Thinker absorbed the data and evaluated it and, asking questions, sought the answers. As if two parts of a computer operating separately, one the memory core that held the programmed data, the other that part of the system which performed the analyzing functions, had been finally brought together—and, now brought together, worked. The pictures were no longer merely something to touch the esthetic sense, but now held a deeper and a greater meaning, the jigsaw pieces gathered from all parts of the universe and flung on the tabletop, waiting there to be put together, to form a pattern, the many tiny, fragmented keys to what might prove to be a single overriding universal plan.

Three minds trembled, poised tiptoe on the brink that opened out into the soul-wrenching gulf of all eternity. Shaken, unable at first to grasp the implications of the possibility that all the answers to all the questions which ever had been asked might be within their grasp, that a totaling up of the secrets of the stars might yield finally the equations of understanding which would allow one to write a single sentence and say: This is the universe.

But the time clock inside one of the minds rang the loud alarm and the insistent summons and it was time to go back to the ship again. There was no denying the cleverness which the men on earth had wrought and the body of the Quester went back to the ship. Back to the ship to empty out the mind of the simulated human and then it would be time for the ship to leap into the sky again and head out for other stars. To go from star to star, to send out the simulated human time and time again in the bodies of intelligences that might be found on other planets and thus to gain, from first hand observation, the information that would enable men, in another day, to deal with these intelligences to mankind's best advantage.

But when Changer came back to the ship, something had gone wrong. Something had happened.

One microsecond of warning that there was something wrong, then a nothingness—a nothingness till now. A half-awakening, but with only one awake, awake and very puzzled. But now, finally, after a time, the three of them together once again, blood brothers of the mind.

—Changer, they were afraid of us. They found out what we were.

—Yes, Quester. Or perhaps they only thought so. They couldn't know it all. They could only guess. A quiver on a dial. A seepage of a current . . .

—But they didn't wait, said Quester. They didn't take a chance. They saw there was something wrong and then they let us have it. They simply let us have it.

—That, Changer told him, is the way men are.

—Changer, you're a man.

—Thinker, I don't know. You tell me what I am.

Down the hall came the sound of running feet and one voice calling loudly: "It went in there. Kathy said she saw it go in there."

The feet made frantic scuffling turns and white-jacketed internes came boiling through the door.

"Mister," shouted one of them, "did you see a wolf?"

"No," said Blake, "I did not see a wolf."

"There's something damn funny going on," said another interne. "Kathy wouldn't lie. She saw something. It scared the hell . . ."

The first interne advanced threateningly.

"Mister, if you're kidding. If this is some sort of joke . . ."

Panic ran wildly in the other minds, a tidal bore of panic—the panic of minds faced with a threatening situation by aliens in an alien situation. Insecurity, failure of understanding, no basis for the assessment of a situation—

"No!" yelled Blake. "No! No—wait . . ."

But he was too late. The change already had begun, the mind of Quester taking over, and once that had happened, once the change had been triggered into action there was no stopping it.

You fools! Blake cried in his mind. You fools! You fools!

The internes surged back, jamming through the door into the corridor.

Facing them stood Quester, his hackles raised, the silver-greyness of his coat shining in the light from the ceiling lamp, crouched to spring, his lips rolled back to reveal the gleaming fangs.

14

Quester crouched and growled, fear rumbling in his throat.

Trapped and no way out. No opening behind or on either side. The only way to go was the opening into the outer tunnel and that was jammed with a howling pack of alien things that walked on two hind legs and were draped in artificial skins. They stank of body and their minds were pouring out at him a brain-wave so intense that it was like a moving wall and he was forced to brace his feet against it. A brain-wave of no intelligence that he could sense, but made up of primal fears and hates that were jumbled and chaotic.

Quester took a slow step forward and the pack shrank back and at that backward movement, he felt a sense of triumph go flaring through his body. Inherited from some remote ancestor, an ancient racial memory buried deep inside his mind burst full-fledged into a warrior-pride and the rumble that was bubbling in his throat erupted into a roaring roll of savage sound—a sound that ripped deep into the alien pack and sent it scattering.

Quester moved. His legs blurred with speed as he leaped into the tunnel and made a quick turn to the right. One of the alien creatures lunged out from the wall toward him, a weapon of some sort raised above its head, poised for the downward stroke. Quester flung himself off stride to close in on the creature. His massive head swung, slashing, a swift and terrible slash that struck the flesh and ripped it and left a tottering creature that screamed as it collapsed.

Quester spun around and faced the creatures that were charging him. His toenails clawed great scratches in the floor and he hurled himself full-speed at the pack. His head swung right and left and his teeth met flesh and tore and the tunnel seemed to fill with the red haze of his rage.

The creatures all were fleeing now except for those upon the floor and some of these were crawling while others only lay and moaned.

Quester skidded to a halt and half-sitting, his back legs bent, but his hindquarters not quite upon the floor, threw up his head and bayed—a cry of triumph and of challenge, the old, unknown-till-now ancestral cry of triumph and of challenge, that in olden days had rung across that far-off planet or drifted sand and snow.

The tunnel was blotted out and he seemed to smell again the clean, dry air of home rather than the strange stinks of this place where he found himself. And he was, most strangely, a very ancient Quester, one of the old proud warrior race that in other days had battled far and deadly against the hordes of now almost forgotten scaly things which had contested with the Questers the dominance of the planet.

Then the odor of the place and its closeness and the harshness of the bright lights shattered off the walls, swept away the sense of other time and place and he rose to his feet again and swung about, uncertainly. The tunnel was clear ahead, but far behind there were creatures running and the air was clogged and murky with the fragmented, but massive mind-waves that came from all directions.

—Changer!

—The stairs, Quester. Get going for those stairs.

—Stairs?

—The door. The closed opening. The one with the sign above it. The little square with the red characters enclosed.

—I see it. But the door is solid.

—Push it. It will open. Use your arms and not your body. Please, remember. Use your arms. You use them so seldom that you forget you have them.

Quester leaped toward the door.

—Your arms, you fool! Your arms!

Quester struck it with his body. It yielded on one side and he slipped quickly through. He was in a cubicle and in the floor of the cubicle was a path of narrow ledges that went downward. Those would be the stairs, he told himself.

He went down them, cautiously at first, then faster as he caught the knack. He came to another cubicle and across the short space of the floor, other stairs led downward.

—Changer?

—Go down them. Go down three sets of them. Then go out the door. It leads into a room, a large room. There'll be many creatures there. Go straight ahead until you reach a large opening to your left. Go out that opening and you will be outdoors.

—Outdoors?

—On the surface of the planet. Outside the building (the cave) that we are in. They have caves on top of the ground here.

—Then what?

—Then run!

—Changer, why don't you take over? You can handle it. You are like these creatures. You can just walk out.

—I can't. I haven't any clothes.

—The coverings? The artificial skins?

—That's right.

—But that is silly. Clothes . . .

—No one stirs anywhere without them. It is the custom.

—And you are bound by custom?

—Look, you'll take the creatures by surprise. For a moment they'll be frozen at the sight of you. Just staring, not doing anything. You resemble a wolf and . . .

—You said that before. I do not like the thought. There is something dirty . . .

—A creature now extinct. A fearsome creature that struck terror into the hearts of people. They'll be frightened when they see you.

—O.K., O.K., O.K. Thinker, how about it?

—You two go ahead, said Thinker. I have no data. I cannot be of help. We must rely on Changer. This is his planet and he knows it.

—All right, then. Here I go.

Quester went padding swiftly down the stairs. The thick, metallic sense of fear lay everywhere. The mindwaves pounded on relentlessly.

If we get out of this, thought Quester, if we get out of this . . .

He felt his own fear creeping in upon him, the descending weight of uncertainty and doubt.

—Changer?

—Go ahead. You're doing fine.

He went down the third flight and faced the door.

—This one?

—Yes, and be fast about it. Your arms this time, remember. Your body bumping the door might not open it wide enough. It could fall back and catch you.

Quester squared off, extruding his arms. He bunched his body and flung himself at the door.

—Changer, to the left? The opening on the left?

—Yes. About ten of your body lengths.

Quester's outstretched arms struck the door and

slapped it open. His body catapulted out into the room. He had a confused sense of startled screaming, of open mouths, of creatures moving swiftly and there was the opening to his left. He pivoted and plunged toward it. A pack of creatures, he saw, were coming toward the opening from the outside—more of the strange creatures who peopled this planet, but draped in different kinds of artificial skins. They opened their mouths to shriek at him and lifted their hands, which held black objects which belched sudden flashes of fire, emitting bitter stenches.

Something smashed into metal very close to him and made a hollow whining sound and something else chewed with a crunching sound into a piece of wood. Then Quester, unable to stop even if he had wished, was among the creatures and the old war-cry was thundering through his body, his head jerking and slashing, his hands striking out. In among them for an instant, then through them and away, streaking along the front of the great cave which reared into the sky.

From behind him came sharp reports and some small, but heavy objects which traveled very fast gouged into the floor on which he ran, throwing up fragments of the material of which the floor was made.

It might be night, he thought, for there was no great star in the sky, although there were many distant stars shining in the sky and that was well, he thought, for it was unthinkable for a planet not to carry with it a canopy of stars.

And there were smells, but now the smells were different, not as acrid, not as sharp or harsh as had been in the building, but more pleasant, gentle smells.

Behind him the popping sound continued and tiny things went past him, then he was at the corner of the cave that went up into the sky, and around the corner, still running, remembering that Changer had said that he must run. And enjoying the running, the smooth, sleek slide of muscles, the feeling of the floor on which he ran, solid underneath his pads.

Now, for the first time since it all had started, he had the chance to gather in the aspects of the planet and it seemed, in many ways, a very busy place. And in other ways very strange, indeed. For who had ever heard of a planet that was floored? The floor ran out from the edge of the cave that reared up into the sky—out into the distance as far as he could see. And everywhere he looked there were other caves, stretching upward from the surface, many of them shining with yellow squares of light, and in front of many of them, and in little areas fenced in on the floor were metallic or stony representations of the planet's residents. And why, Quester wondered, should things like this exist? Could it be, he wondered, that when these creatures died, they were turned to metal or to stone and left standing wherever they had died? Although that did not seem reasonable, for many of the creatures turned to stone or metal seemed larger than life size. But it was entirely possible, of course, that the creatures came in many different sizes and perhaps only the larger ones were metamorphosed into stone or metal.

There were not many of the planet's living residents in evidence, and all those a distance off. But moving on the surface of the floor, and very rapidly, were metallic shapes that had glowing eyes on the front of them and that made a whooshing sound and sent out a blast of air as they streaked along. From these metallic shapes came brainwaves, the sense of a living thing, but a living thing that in many cases had more brains than one—and the brain-waves were quiet and gentle, not loaded with the hate and fear that he had sensed back there in the cave.

It was strange, of course, but Quester told himself, it would be unusual if one met only one kind of life upon a planet. So far there had been the things that walked on two hind legs and were protoplasmic, and the metallic things that moved very rapidly and purposefully and shot light from their eyes and had more brains than one. And there had been that other time, he recalled, on that wet, hot night when he had sensed many other forms of life that seemed to hold either poor intelligence or no intelligence, beings that were little more than bundles of matter which held the gift of life.

If only, he thought, this planet were not so hot and its atmosphere not so heavy and oppressive, it might prove very interesting. Although it all was most confusing.

—Quester.

—What is it, Changer?

—Off to your right. The trees. The large vegetation. You can see them against the sky. Head for them. If we can get in among them, they will help to hide us.

—Changer, asked Thinker, what do we do now?

—I don't know. We'll have to think about it. All three of us together.

—These creatures will be hunting us?

—I presume they will.

—We should be one mind. Quester and I should know everything you know.

—We will, said Quester. There has been no time. There has been too much happening. The distractions have been great.

—Reach the trees, said Changer, and we'll have the time.

Quester swerved away from the side of the mighty cave that rose into the sky, cutting out across the wide strip of flooring, heading for the trees. Charging out of the darkness, its two eyes gleaming hard, came one of the metallic creatures, with the soft sighing of its windstorm. It swerved and headed straight for him and Quester flattened out. His legs blurred and his body hugged the bleaming surface of the floor, his ears laid back, his tail pointed straight behind him.

Changer cheered him on.

—Run, you mangy wolf! Run, you haggard jackal! Run, you frantic fox!

15

The chief of staff was a calm and officious man. He was not the kind of man one would expect to bang his fist upon a desk.

But now he banged his fist.

"What I want to know," he bellowed, "is what stupid knothead phoned the police. We could have handled this ourselves. We needed no police."

"I would imagine, sir," said Michael Daniels, "that whoever might have called them thought they had some reason to. The corridor was littered with people all chewed up."

"We could have taken care of them," said the chief of staff. "That is the business we are in. We could have taken care of them and then proceeded in a fashion far more orderly."

"You must realize, sir," said Gordon Barnes, "that everyone must have been upset. A wolf in the . . ."

The chief of staff waved Barnes to silence, spoke to the nurse.

"Miss Gregerson, you were the first to see this thing."

The girl still was pale and frightened, but she nodded. "I came out of a room and it was in the corridor. A wolf. I dropped my tray and screamed and ran. It was a frightening . . ."

"You're sure it was a wolf?"

"Yes, sir, I am sure."

"How could you be sure. It might have been a dog."

"Dr. Winston," Daniels said, "you're trying to confuse the issue. It makes no difference whether it was a wolf or dog."

The chief of staff glared at him angrily, then made an impatient gesture.

"All right," he said. "All right. The rest of you may leave. If you'd be so good as to stay, Dr. Daniels, I would like to talk with you."

The two waited and the others filed out.

"Now, Mike," said the chief of staff, "let the two of us sit down and make some sense of it. Blake was your patient, wasn't he?"

"Yes, he was. You're acquainted with him, doctor. The man who was found in space. Frozen and encapsulated."

"Yes, I know," said Winston. "What did he have to do with this?"

"I'm not sure," said Daniels. "I'd suspect he was the wolf."

Winston made a face. "Come now," he said. "You can't expect me to believe a thing like that. What you are saying is Blake most likely was a werewolf."

"Did you read this evening's papers?"

"No, I can't say I have. What would the papers have to do with what happened here?"

"Nothing, perhaps, but I'm inclined to think . . ."

Daniels stopped what he had meant to say. Good God, he told himself, it is too fantastic. It simply couldn't happen. Although it was the one thing which might explain what had happened up on the third floor an hour or so ago.

"Doctor Daniels, what are you inclined to think? If you have some information, please come forth with it. You realize, of course, what this means to us. Publicity—too much publicity and the wrong kind of it entirely. Sensationalism, and a hospital can't afford sensationalism. I hate to think what, even now, the papers and dimensino may be doing with it. And there'll be a police inquiry. Already they're snooping around the place, talking to people they have no right to talk with and asking questions that should not be asked. And investigations of all sorts. Congressional hearings maybe. Space Administration will be down our throat, wanting to know what happened to Blake, to this prize pet of theirs. And I can't tell them, Daniels, that he turned into a wolf."

"Not a wolf, sir. But an alien creature. One that looks remarkably like a wolf. You'll recall the police claimed it was a wolf with arms sprouting from its shoulders."

The chief of staff growled. "No one else said that. The police were panicked. Shooting straight into the lobby. One bullet missed the receptionist by no more than inches. Crashed into the paneling just above her head. They were frightened men, I tell you. They don't know what they saw. What was this you were saying about an alien creature?"

Daniels drew in a deep breath and took the plunge. "A witness by the name of Lukas testified this afternoon at the bioengineering hearing. He'd dug up some old record about two simulated men being processed a couple of centuries ago. Claimed he found the records in the Space Administration files . . ."

"Why those files? Why should a record of that sort . . ."

"Wait," said Daniels. "You haven't heard the half of it. These were open-ended androids . . ."

"Good Lord!" exclaimed Winston. He stared glassily at Daniels. "The old werewolf principle! An organism that could change, that could be anything at all. There is that old myth . . ."

"Apparently it wasn't a myth," said Daniels, grimly. "Two of the androids were synthesized and sent out on survey and exploration ships."

"And you think Blake is one of them?"

"That's the thought I had. Lukas testified this afternoon that the two went out. The records then are silent. No mention of their coming back."

"It just doesn't make good sense," protested Winston. "Good Lord, man, two hundred years ago. If they made androids then, good, serviceable androids, we'd be swarming with them now. You just don't make two of anything and then drop the entire project."

"You would," said Daniels, "if those two didn't work. Let's say, just for argument, that not only the androids failed to return, but likewise the ships that they were on. That they just blasted off into nothingness and there was no further word of them. Not only would no more of the androids be made, but the record of the failure would be buried deep inside the files. It wouldn't be anything that Space Administration would want someone digging out."

"But they couldn't know the androids had anything to do with the disappearance of the ships. In the old days, and even now, there are ships that don't come back."

Daniels shook his head. "One ship maybe. Anything could happen to a single ship. But two ships with one thing in common, each ship with an android aboard—then it wouldn't take anyone long to figure the android might have been the reason. Or that the android set up a certain circumstance . . ."

"I don't like it," complained the chief of staff. "I don't like the smell of it. I don't want to get tangled up with Space. They swing a lot of weight and they wouldn't like it if we tried to pin it onto them. And, anyhow, I don't see how all this would tie up with Blake turning, as you seem to think, into a wolf."

"I told you once before," said Daniels. "Not a wolf. Into an alien that has the appearance of a wolf. Say the werewolf principle didn't work the way it was thought it would. The android was intended to turn into an alien form, utilizing the data extracted from a captured alien and to live as that alien for a time. Then the alien data would be erased and the android would be a man again, ready to be changed into something else. But suppose . . ."

"I see," said Winston. "Suppose it didn't work. Suppose the alien data couldn't be erased. Suppose the android stayed both alien and human—two creatures and either one it wished."

"That, sir," said Daniels, "is what I had been thinking. And there is something else. We took an electro-encephalogram of Blake and it showed up something strange. As if he had more minds than one. Like shadows of other minds showing in the tracings."

"Shadows? You mean more than one extra mind?"

"I don't know," said Daniels. "The indications were not pronounced. Nothing that you could be sure of."

Winston got up from behind the desk and paced up and down the floor.

"I hope you're wrong," he said. "I think you are. It's crazy."

"It's one way," Daniels told him, stubbornly, "that we can explain what happened."

"But one thing we don't explain. Blake was found frozen, in a capsule. No sign of the ship. No other debris. How do we figure that one out?"

"We don't," said Daniels. "There is no way that we can. We can't know what happened. When you talk about debris, you are presuming the ship was destroyed and we don't know if that happened. Even if it had been, over a couple of centuries the debris would have drifted apart. It might even have been in the vicinity of the capsule and not been seen. In space, visibility is poor. Unless something picks up light and reflects it, you wouldn't know that it was there."

"You think perhaps the crew got onto what had happened and grabbed Blake and froze him, then shot him out into space inside the capsule? One way of getting rid of him? An unmessy way to do it?"

"I wouldn't know, sir. There is no way that we can know. All we can do is speculate and there are too many areas of speculation for us to be certain we have concentrated on the right one. If the crew did what you said, getting rid of Blake, then why didn't the ship come back. You explain one thing and then you have another to explain and perhaps another and another. It would seem a hopeless task to me."

Winston stopped his pacing, came back to the desk and sat down in the chair. He reached out his hand for the communicator.

"What was the name of this man who testified?"

"Lukas. Dr. Lukas. I don't recall his first name. It would be in the papers. The switchboard operator more than likely has one."

"I suppose we'd better get the senators down here, too, if they can come. Horton—Chandler Horton. Who is the other one?"

"Solomon Stone."

"O.K.," said Winston, "we'll see what they think of this. Them and Lukas."

"Space, too, sir?"

Winston shook his head. "No. Not right at the moment. We'll need more to go on before we start tangling with Space."

16

The den was small and close—a projecting ledge of rock with a space eroded out beneath it. Above it the ground rose sharply, below it the ground fell steeply away. At the foot of the hill a stream of water ran raggedly over a pebbly bed. On the slope at the lip of the cave the ground was littered with tiny slabs of rock—the shards that through the years had been eroded out of the face of the stone. The slabs shifted treacherously under Quester's paws as he scrambled for the cave, but he managed to squeeze himself into it, twisting around until he could face outward.

For the first time now he felt a measure of safety, with his flanks and back protected, but he knew that it was an illusory safety. The creatures of this planet, even now, perhaps, were hunting him and it would not be long, he was certain, before they'd be combing through the area. Certainly he had been seen by the metallic creature which had come charging after him with its howling windstorm and its glaring eyes that shot out light before it. He shuddered as he recalled how he had barely gained the shelter of the trees just ahead of it. Another three lengths of his body to have gone and it would have overrun him.

He relaxed, willing his body to grow limp in every muscle.

His mind went out, checking, seeking, prying. There was life, more life than one would expect—an overcrowded planet, a place that swarmed with life. Tiny resting life, unthinking, unintelligent, existing but doing little more. There were small intelligences that rustled, restless, alert, afraid—but their intelligence so thin and barren that they were little more than aware of life and the dangers that might threaten it. One thing ran, seeking, hunting, with the red streak of killing pulsating in its mind, vicious and terrible and a very hungry thing. Three life forms were huddled in one place, some safe and hidden place, for their minds were snug and smug and warm. And others—many, many others. Life and some of the life with intelligence. But nowhere the sharp, bright, terrifying sense of the things that lived in the above-ground caves.

A messy planet, thought Quester, untidy and unneat, with too much life and water and too much vegetation, its air too thick and heavy and its climate far too hot. A place that gave one no rest at all, no sense of security, the sort of place where one must sense and watch and listen and fear that, even so, an undetected danger might come slipping through the net and fasten on one's throat. The trees were moaning gently and he wondered, as he listened to them, if it were the trees themselves, or if the moaning came from the moving atmosphere that was blowing through them.

And as he lay there wondering, he knew that it was the friction of the wind against the substance of the trees and the rustling of the leaves, the groaning of the branches, that the trees themselves had no way to make a sound, that the trees and all the other vegetation upon this planet, which was called the Earth, were alive, but with no intelligence and no perceptive senses. And that the caves were buildings and that the humans were not tribal members, but formed sexual units which were known as families, and that a building in which a family lived was called a home.

The information bore down upon him like a tidal wave

that curled above him and overwhelmed him in a moment of blind panic and he came battling out of it and the tidal wave was gone. But in his mind, he knew, lay all the knowledge of the planet, every shred of information which lay in the mind of Changer.

—I am sorry, Changer said. There was no time for you to absorb it slowly and decently and get acquainted with it and try to classify it. I gave it all at once. Now you have it all to use.

Tentatively, Quester took a quick survey of it and shuddered at the tangled pile it was.

—Much of it is out of date, said Changer. There are many things that I don't know. You have this planet as I knew it two hundred years ago, plus what I picked up since I returned to it. I would impress upon you that the data are not complete and some of it may now be worthless.

Quester crouched close against the rock floor of the den, still probing out into the darkness of the woods, straightening and strengthening the detection net that he had laid out in all directions.

A since of desolation swept through him. Homesickness for the planet of drifted snow and sand—and no way to get back. Perhaps never to get back. Here in this tangled place of too much life and too much danger and not knowing where to turn, not knowing what to do. Hunted by the dominant creatures of the planet, creatures that he now knew were more horrible than he had thought they were. Cunning and ruthless and illogical, weighed down by fears and hatreds, obeying the murderous drive of a species on the make.

—Changer, he asked, what of my other body? The one I inhabited before you humans came. You caught that body, I remember. What did you do with it?

—Not I! I didn't catch it. I did nothing with it.

—Don't try your human legalistic tricks on me. Don't

take refuge in semantics. Not you alone, perhaps. Not you personally, but . . .

—Quester, Thinker said, don't take that tone of thought. The three of us are caught in a single trap—if it is a trap. I'm inclined to believe it may not be a trap, but a unique situation which will work to our advantage. We share one body and our minds are closer than any minds have ever been before. And we must not quarrel; we must not have differences, for we can't afford them. We must work together always. We must harmonize ourselves. If there are differences, we must work them out immediately, we must not let them fester.

—That, said Quester, is exactly what I'm doing. There is a thing that bothers me. What happened to that first me?

—That first body, Changer told him, was biologically scanned. It was taken apart, almost molecule by molecule, and analyzed. There was no way in which it could be reassembled.

—You murdered me, you mean.

—If you want to call it that.

—And Thinker, too?

—Thinker, too. Thinker was the first.

—Thinker, Quester asked, do you not resent this?

—What good would resentment accomplish?

—That is no answer and you know it.

—I can't be sure, said Thinker. I would have to cogitate it. One must, of course, resent any violence done him. But I would be inclined to consider what has happened as a transfiguration rather than a violence. If this had not occurred to me I could never have existed in your body or touched your mind. All the data that you gathered from the stars would have been lost to me and lost most piti-fully, for I'd never have known of it. And you, in turn, if it had not been for what the humans did, never would have guessed the significance of the pictures that you garnered from the stars. You simply would have gone on garnering them and enjoying them and perhaps not even wondered at them and I can conceive of nothing more tragic than that, to be on the edge of mystery and not even wonder at it.

—I am not so sure, said Quester, that I would prefer the mystery and forego the wonder.

—But don't you see the beauty of it? Thinker asked. Here the three of us, all of us most different. Three types most distinctive. You, Quester, the roughneck and the bandit, Changer the cunning schemer, and I . . .

—And you, said Quester, the all-wise, the far-seeing . . .

—I was about to say, said Thinker, the fumbler after truth.

—If it will make either of you feel better, Changer told them, I'll apologize for the human race. In many ways I like them no better than you do.

—For good reason, Thinker said. For you are not human. You are something made by humans, you are an agent of the humans.

—And yet, said Changer, one must be something. I'd rather be a human than not anything at all. One cannot stand alone.

—You will not be alone, said Thinker. The two of us are with you.

—Still, said Changer stubbornly, I insist on being human.

—I cannot understand, said Thinker.

—Perhaps I can, said Quester. Back there in the hospital I felt something I had not felt before, something that no quester has felt for a long, long time. The pride of race, and, furthermore, a pride in the racial fighting spirit that was tucked away somewhere deep inside of me and that I had not known was there. I suspect, Changer, that my race, in the time of long ago, was as much upon the prod as your race is today. And it is a prideful thing to be of such a race. It gives you strength and stature and a great deal of self-respect. It is something that Thinker and his kind perhaps could never feel.

—My pride, if I had any, Thinker said, would be of a different kind and arise from different motives. But I will not foreclose there being many kinds of pride.

Quester jerked his attention to the hillside and the woods, alerted by a whiff of danger that had come snaking along the detection net that he had laid out.

—Quiet! he told the other two.

Faint, far off, he caught the indications and zeroed in on them. There were three of them, three humans, and in a little time more than three of them—a long line of them advancing cautiously, searching through the woods. And there could be, he knew, only one thing that they sought.

He caught the faint edges of their mind-waves and they were afraid, but they were also angry and filled with a hate-tinged loathing. But as well as this fear and hatred, there was the sense of hunt, the strange, wild excitement that drove them on to find and kill the thing that was the cause of fear.

Quester bunched his body and half-rose to dart out of the den. For there was, he thought, only one way to elude these humans—to run and run and run.

—Wait, said Thinker.

—They will be on top of us.

—Not for a time. They are moving slowly. There may be a better way. We cannot run forever. We have made one mistake. We should not make another.

—What mistake?

—We should not have changed to you. We should have stayed as Changer. It was blind panic that forced us to make the change.

—But we had no knowledge. We saw danger and reacted. We were being threatened . . .

—I could have bluffed it out, said Changer. But this way may have been the best at that. They had suspicions of me. They would have put me under observation. They might have locked me up. This way, at least, we're free.

—But not for long, said Thinker, if we keep on running. There are too many of them—too many on the planet. We can't hide from all of them. We can't dodge them all. Mathematically we have so little chance that it is no chance at all.

—You have something in your mind? asked Quester.

—Why don't we change to me. I can be a lump, a nothing, something in this cave. A rock, perhaps. When they look into it they will see nothing strange.

—A minute, there, said Changer. Your idea is all right, but there may be problems.

—Problems?

—You should have it figured out by now. Not problems, but a problem. The climate of this planet. It is too warm for Quester. It will be far too cold for you.

—Cold is lack of heat?

—That's right.

—Lack of energy?

—Correct.

—It takes a little time to get all the terminology sorted out, said Thinker. It has to be catalogued, soaked into the mind. But I can stand some cold. For the common cause I can stand a lot of cold.

—It's not just a matter of standing it. Of course, you can do that. But you require great amounts of energy.

—When I formed that time in the house . . .

—You had the energy supply of the house to draw on. Here there is nothing but the heat stored in the atmosphere. And now that the sun is down, that is steadily becoming less and less. You'll have to operate on the energy that the body has. You can't draw on outside sources.

—I see, said Thinker. But I can form a shape to conserve what energy there is. I can hug it to me. If the change is made, I have all the energy that is in the body?

—I would think you would have. The change itself perhaps requires some energy exchange, but I suspect not very much.

—How do you feel, Quester?

—Hot, said Quester.

—I don't mean that. You aren't tired, are you? No lack of energy?

—I feel all right, said Quester.

—We wait, said Thinker, until they are almost here. Then we change to me and I am a nothing or almost a nothing. Just a shapeless lump. Best way would be for me to spread myself all around the cave, a lining for the cave. But that way I'd lose too much energy.

—They may not see the cave, said Changer. They may pass it by.

—We can't take chances, Thinker said. I'll be me no longer than we have to. We must change back as soon as they are past. If what you say is true.

—Calculate it for yourself, invited Changer. You have the data that I gave you. You know as much physics, as much chemistry as I do.

—The data, perhaps, Changer. But not the habit of mind to employ it. Not your way of thought. Not your ability at mathematics, not your swift grasp of universal principles.

—But you are our thinker.

—I think another way.

—Stop this jabbering, Quester said, impatiently. Let's get set what we are to do. Once they're past, we change back to me.

—No, said Changer. Back to me.

—But you haven't any clothes.

—Out here it doesn't matter.

—Your feet. You need shoes. There are rocks and sticks.
And your eyes are no good in the dark.

—They are almost here, warned Thinker.

—That is right, said Quester. They are coming down the
hill.

17

It was fifteen minutes until her favorite dimensino program came on. Elaine Horton had looked forward to it all day, for Washington was boring. Already she was looking forward to the time when she could return to the old stone house in the Virginia hills.

She sat down and picked up a magazine and was idly flipping through its pages when the senator came in.

"What did you do all day?" he asked.

"Part of the time I watched the hearing."

"Good show?"

"Fairly interesting. What I can't understand is why you bothered to dig up that stuff from two hundred years ago."

He chuckled. "Well, partly, I suppose, to shake up Stone. I couldn't see his face. I would guess his eyeballs might have popped."

"Mostly," she said, "he simply sat there glaring. I suppose that you were proving that bioengineering is not so new a thing as many people think."

He sat down in a chair and picked up a paper, glanced at the glaring headlines.

"That," he said, "and that it can be done—that it, in fact, was being done, and rather skillfully, two centuries ago. And that we were scared out once, but shouldn't be again. Think of all the time we've lost—two hundred years of time. I have other witnesses who will point that out, rather forcefully."

He shook out the paper and settled down to read.

"Your mother get away all right?" he asked.

"Yes, she did. The plane left a little before noon."

"Rome this time, isn't it. Was it films or poetry or what?"

"Films this time. Some old prints someone found from the end of the twentieth century, I believe."

The senator sighed. "Your mother," he told her, "is an intelligent woman. She appreciates such things; I'm afraid I don't. She was talking about taking you along with her. It might have been interesting if you had cared to go."

"You know it wouldn't have been interesting," she said. "You are an old fraud. You make noises as if you admired these things that Mother likes, but you don't care a lick."

"I guess you're right," he agreed. "What's on dimensino? Could I squeeze in the booth with you?"

"There is plenty of room and you know it. And you would be very welcome. I'm waiting for Horatio Alger. It will be on in another ten minutes or so."

"Horatio Alger—what is that?"

"I guess you'd call it a serial. It goes on and on. Horatio Alger is the man who wrote it. He wrote a lot of books, back in the early part of the twentieth century, maybe before that. The critics then thought they were trashy books and I suppose they were. But a lot of people read them and that apparently meant that they had some sort of human appeal. They told all about how a poor boy makes good against terrific odds."

"It sounds sort of corny to me," said the senator.

"I suppose it does. But the producers and the writers have taken those trashy stories and turned them into social documents, with a good bit of satire laced into the story. And they have done a marvellous job of recreating the background, the most of it I suppose is the late nine-teenth century and the early twentieth. And not just the physical background, but the moral and social background. It was a barbarous age, you know. There are human situations in it that make your blood run cold . . ."

The phone beeped at them and the vision panel blinked.

The senator hoisted himself from the chair and crossed the room.

Elaine settled more comfortably in her chair. Five minutes more to go before the program would come on. And it would be nice to have the senator join her in watching. She hoped that nothing happened to prevent him joining her. Like that phone call, for instance. She flipped the pages of the magazine. Back of her she heard the mumbled voices of the conversation.

The senator came back.

"I'll have to go out for a while," he said.

"You'll miss Horatio."

He shook his head. "I'll catch it some other time. That was Ed Winston, down at St. Barnabas."

"The hospital. Anything wrong?"

"No one hurt. No one ill. If that is what you mean. But Winston seemed upset. Said he had to see me. Wouldn't tell me what was going on."

"You won't stay out too long. Get back early if you can. With these hearings, you need sleep."

"I'll do my best," he said.

She went to the front door with him, helped him with his cloak, then came back into the living room.

The hospital, she thought. She didn't like the sound of it. What could the senator possibly have to do with a hospital? Hospitals made her edgy. She had gone to that very hospital just this afternoon and she hadn't wanted to, but she was glad she had. That poor guy, she thought, is really in a jam. Not knowing who he is, not knowing what he is.

She went into the dimensino booth and sat down in a

chair, the curving screen glinting in front of her and on either side. She pressed the buttons and turned the dial and the screen began its preliminary flicker.

Strange, she thought, how her mother could get excited about an ancient piece of film—an old, flat, two-dimensional entertainment medium that most people had forgotten ever had existed. And the worst of it, she thought wryly, was that people who professed to see something of great value in the old-time things also professed a great contempt for modern entertainment as devoid of all art. In a few hundred years, perhaps, when new entertainment mediums had evolved, the old dimensino would be rediscovered as an ancient art that had not been properly appreciated at the time it flourished.

The screen quit its flickering and she seemed to stand in a downtown street.

A voice said: ". . . no one yet can give an explanation of what happened here less than an hour ago. There are conflicting reports and no two stories absolutely check. The hospital is beginning to calm down now, but for a time there was pandemonium. There are reports that one of the patients is missing, but the reports can't be confirmed. Most accounts agree that some animal, some say it was a wolf, went raging through the corridors, attacking everyone who stood in its way. One story is that the wolf, if wolf it was, had arms that sprouted from its shoulders. The police, when they arrived, fired at something, spraying the reception room with bullets . . ."

Elaine caught her breath. St. Barnabas! This was St. Barnabas. She had gone there to see Andrew Blake and her father now was on his way there—and what was going on?

She half-rose from her chair, then sat down again. There was nothing she could do or should do. The senator would be able to look out for himself; he always had. And whatever had been in the hospital now was gone, or apparently it was. If she waited just a little while, she'd see her father get out of the car and walk up the stairs.

She stood and shivered in the chill wind that was sweeping down the street.

18

The footsteps sounded near, slipping and sliding on the shards of stone that lay outside the cave mouth. A beam of light speared into the cave.

Thinker pulled himself tighter and denser and reduced his field. The field might betray him, he knew, but he could not reduce it much further, even so, for it was a part of him and he could not exist without it. Especially not here, not at this moment, with the chill of the atmosphere sucking hungrily at his energy.

We must be ourselves, he thought. I, myself, and Quester quester's self and Changer changer's self. We cannot be more or less than we are and we cannot change except through the process of long, slow evolution, but in the millenia to come might it not be possible that the three would meld as one, that there would not be three separate minds, but one mind only? And that mind would have emotion, which I do not have, which I can recognize, but cannot understand, and the hard, cold, impersonal logic which is mine, but not my companions', and the keen sharp sensitivity which is Quester's, but is neither mine nor Changer's. Blind chance alone that put the three of us together, that put our minds inside a mass of matter which can be made a body—what were the odds that such a happening could have come about? Blind chance or destiny? What was destiny? Was there destiny? Could there be some great, over-riding universal plan and was this happening which had put the three of them together one part of that plan, a necessary step before the plan could reach that remote conclusion toward which it always moved?

The human was crawling closer, the loose rock sliding underneath his feet, his hands clawing at the ground to hold himself against the downhill pull of gravity, the lighted flashlight in one fist bobbing and bouncing so that it threw an erratic arc of light.

He got one elbow over the lip of the cave and hoisted himself upward so that his head was level with the opening.

He gasped and yelled.

"Hey, Bob, this cave has a funny smell. There's been something in here. Just a while ago."

Thinker expanded his field, pushing it outward violently. It hit the man like a plunging fist. It knocked his elbow loose from the lip of rock and hurled him outward and away. He twisted and plunged downward. He screamed once, a shriek of terror pushed out of his lungs. Then his body thumped and slid. Thinker could sense its sliding, taking with it rocks that bounced and clicked, trash wood that slithered and rattled. The slithering and the clicking stopped and from the slope below came the sound of splashing.

Thrashing bodies went plunging down the slope, lights bobbing back and forth, sweeping across brush and shiny tree trunks.

Voices cried out:

"Bob, something happened to Harry!"

"Yeah, I heard him yell."

"He's down there in the creek. I heard him hit the water."

The plunging bodies kept on going past, going down the hill in braking rushes. A half a dozen lights bobbed madly at the bottom of the slope and several of the humans were wading in the stream. From farther off came other shouts.

Something stirred questioningly inside Thinker's mind.
—Yes, he asked, what is it?

—What do we do now? growled Quester. You heard what he yelled. They're all excited now, but one of them will remember. There'll be some of them coming up here. They may start shooting at us.

—I agree, said Changer. They'll investigate. The man who fell . . .

—Fell! said Thinker, witheringly. I pushed him.

—All right, then. The man you pushed tipped them off. He smelled Quester, maybe.

—I don't stink, said Quester.

—That's ridiculous, said Thinker. I would suspect all three of us have distinctive body odors. Your body form was there long enough to contaminate the cave.

—It might have been your body odor, said Quester. Don't forget . . .

—Cut it out, said Changer, sharply. The question isn't which one of us he smelled. It is what do we do now. Thinker, can you change into something thin and flat, a shape that will give no profile, and creep out of here and up the hill?

—I doubt it. The planet's far too cold. I'm losing energy too fast. If I extended my body surface I'd lose it that much faster.

—That's a problem that we have to face, said Quester. The problem of retaining sufficient energy. Changer will have to eat for us. He'll have to supply the energy, ingesting in his own body form the foods that are available. And staying in his body's form long enough for the food to be digested. There are few energy sources for Thinker and probably no food that I could eat and that my bodily apparatus would be able to handle. I would suspect . . .

—This all is true, said Changer. But let's consider it some other time. For the moment, let's go back to our present problem. Can you take over, Quester? They'd spot me. My body would show up white.

—Certainly I can, said Quester.

—Good. Crawl out of the cave and up the hill. Go easily, go quietly. But as swiftly as you can. We've got the searching party all together and if they don't hear you, it's unlikely we'll run into any of them.

—Over the hill, asked Quester, and then what?

—Up on one of the drives, said Changer, we should find a public telephone.

19

"If what you believe is true," Chandler Horton said, "then we must lose no time in contacting Blake."

"What makes you think it's Blake any longer?" asked the chief of staff. "It wasn't Blake that ran off from this hospital. If Daniels is right, it was an alien creature."

"But Blake was there, too," protested Horton. "It might have been in an alien's body, but it could change back to Blake."

Senator Stone, hunched up in the big chair, sneered at Horton. "If you want to know what I think," he said, "this all is poppycock."

"We are interested in your thoughts, of course," said Horton. "But I do wish, Solomon, that for once your thinking could be a bit constructive."

"What is there to be constructive about?" yelled Stone. "This is some sort of childish, put-up job. I haven't got it figured out yet, but I know that is what it is. And I'll wager you're at the bottom of it, Chandler. You're always up to tricks. You've got this deal rigged up to prove something, more than likely, but so far I don't quite see what it is. I knew there was something going on when you got this Lukas joker up to testify."

"Dr. Lukas, if you don't mind, senator," said Horton.

"Well, all right then. Dr. Lukas. What does he know about it?"

"Let's find out," said Horton. "Dr. Lukas, what do you know about it?"

Lukas grinned drily. "As to what happened in this hos-

pital, not a thing at all. As to whether it could happen as
Dr. Daniels believes it could—why, I must agree with
him."

"But it's supposition," Stone pointed out. "Nothing but
supposition. Dr. Daniels got it figured out. Fine! Good!
Bully for him! He's got a good imagination. But it doesn't
mean that what he thinks is actually what happened."

"I must point out to you," said the chief of staff, "that
Blake was Dr. Daniels' patient."

"Which means you believe what he thinks?"

"Not necessarily. I don't know what to think. But if
anyone is entitled to any opinion, it is Daniels here."

"Now let's all calm down a bit," suggested Horton,
"and take a look at what we have. I scarcely think it's
necessary to dignify the senator's charges that this is a
put-up job with any sort of answer, but I think we must
all agree that something most unusual did happen here
tonight. I also doubt that the decision by Dr. Winston to
call us all together was one that was lightly made. He
now says he can form no solid opinion, but certainly he
must have felt there was some reason for concern."

"I still think there is," said the chief of staff.

"I understand the wolf, or whatever it was . . ."

Solomon Stone gave an explosive snort.

Horton stared at him icily. "Or whatever it was," he
continued, "ran across the street into the park and the
police gave chase."

"That's right," said Daniels. "They're out there now,
trying to hunt it down. Some damn fool of a motorist
caught it in his headlights when it crossed the road and
tried to run it down."

"Don't you see," said Horton, "that this is the sort of
thing we have to stop. Everyone around here apparently
went off half-cocked . . ."

"You must understand," explained the chief of staff,

"that it all was fairly frantic. No one was thinking straight."

"If Blake is what Daniels thinks he is," said Horton, "we have to get him back. We lost two centuries of progress in human bioengineering because it was believed the Space Administration project failed and because of that the project was hushed up. Hushed up so effectively, I might point out, that it was forgotten. All that remained of it was a myth and legend. But now it appears that it didn't fail. We may have evidence of its success out there in the woods right now."

"Oh, it failed, all right," said Lukas. "It didn't work the way that Space had meant it to. I think Daniels has the right hunch. Once the characteristics of an alien were fed into the android, they couldn't be erased. They became a permanent feature of the android itself. He became two creatures—the human and an alien. In everything. In bodily characteristics and in mental setup."

"This mental situation, sir," asked the chief of staff. "Would the android's mentality have been synthetic? By that I mean a carefully worked-out mentality that was synthesized and fed into it."

Lukas shook his head. "I would doubt that, doctor. It would have been a crude method, a rather silly way to go about it. The records, or at least the ones I've seen, make no mention of it, but I would presume that the pattern of an actual human mind was impressed upon its brain. Even then they would have had the technique for it. The mind-banks were created how long ago?"

"A bit over three hundred years ago," said Horton.

"Then they would have had the technique for such a transfer. And this business of building up a synthetic mind would be difficult today, let alone two hundred years ago. Even now I would doubt that we'd know all the ingredients to provide a balanced mind—one that would be human. There is so much that goes to make a human mind. We could synthesize a mind—yes, I suppose we could—but a strange one, giving rise to strange actions, strange emotions, not entirely human, something less than human, perhaps something more than human."

"So you think," said Horton, "that Blake carries around in his brain the duplication of the mind of a man who lived at the time he was fabricated."

"I would be almost positive of it," said Lukas.

"So would I," said the chief of staff.

"So then," said Horton, "he really is a human—or, at least, he has a human mind?"

"I see no other way," said Lukas, "in which they could have provided him a mind."

"It's all poppycock," said Senator Stone. "I've never heard so much damn foolishness in all my born days."

No one paid attention to him.

The chief of staff looked at Horton. "You believe it's vital that we get Blake back?"

"I do," said Horton. "Before the police kill him or it or whatever body he may be occupying. Before they drive him into so deep a hole to hide that it will take months to find him, if we ever do."

"I agree," said Lukas. "Think of all he'd have to tell us. Think of what we could learn by a study of him. If the Earth expects to embark on a program of human-engineering, either now or at some future time, what we could learn from Blake would be invaluable."

The chief of staff shook his head, bewildered. "But Blake's a special case. An open-ended specimen. As I understand it, the proposed bioengineering program did not envision such a creature."

"Doctor," said Lukas, "what you say is true, but any kind of android, any kind of organized synthetic . . ."

"You gentlemen are wasting your time," said Stone. "There isn't going to be a human bioengineering program. I and some of my colleagues are about to see to that."

"Solomon," said Horton, patiently, "let's you and I worry about the politics of the issue later. Right now we have a frightened man out there in the woods and we have to find some way to let him know we don't mean him any harm."

"And how do you propose doing that?"

"Why, it seems simple to me. Call off the hunt, then release the news. Have the newspapers and the electronic media in and . . ."

"You think a wolf will read a newspaper or watch dimensino?"

"He wouldn't stay a wolf, most likely," Daniels said. "I have a hunch that as soon as possible, he'll turn back into a man. For one thing, an alien creature might find this planet confusing and uncomfortable."

"Gentlemen," said the chief of staff. "Please, gentlemen."

They all turned to look at him.

"We can't do that," he said. "Such a story would make the hospital appear ridiculous. It would be bad enough in any instance, but the werewolf connotations! Can't you see the headlines? Can't you see the holiday the press would have at our expense?"

"But if we were right?" asked Daniels.

"That's the point. We can't know that we are right. We might have all the reason in the world to believe that we were right, but that still wouldn't be enough. On a thing like this, we must be dead certain and we can't be that."

"Then you refuse to let such an announcement be made?"

"So far as the hospital is concerned, I can't. If Space would give clearance to it, then I would agree. But I can't, not on my own. Even if I were right, Space would be down on me like a ton of bricks. They'd raise holy hell . . ."

"Even after two hundred years?"

"Even after that long a time. Can't you see that if Blake is what we think he is, he belongs to Space? It's up to them. He is their baby, not mine. He is something that they started and . . ."

Stone's chuckle rumbled through the room.

"Don't pay any attention to him, Chandler. Go ahead and tell the newspaper boys yourself. Go on and break the story. Show us you have some guts. Follow your convictions. I just hope you do."

"I just bet you do," said Horton.

"If you do," said Stone, "I warn you, friend. One public word from you and I'll blow you so far out of the water it'll take you two weeks to come down."

20

The steady beeping of the phone finally beat its way into the illusion-world bounded by dimensino. Elaine Horton roused herself, came out of the booth in which she had been sitting with the shadow-world of ancient days going on about her.

The phone kept up its beeping, the vision panel flashing in impatient pulses.

She made her way to it and switched it to receive. A face looked out at her, faintly lighted by a defective light bulb in the ceiling of a public phone booth.

"Andrew Blake?" she cried, surprised.

"Yes, it's me. You see . . ."

"Is there something wrong? The senator was called down to the . . ."

"I seem to be in a bit of trouble," Blake told her. "You probably heard what happened."

"At the hospital, you mean. I watched it for a while, but there wasn't much to see. Something about a wolf and they said one of the patients seems to have disappeared . . ."

She drew her breath in sharply. "One of the patients disappeared! Did they mean you, Andrew?"

"I'm afraid they did. And I need some help. And you're the only one I know, the only one that I could ask. . . ."

"What kind of help?" she asked.

"I need some clothes," he told her.

"You mean you left the hospital without any clothes? And it's cold out there. . . ."

"It's a long story," he said. "If you don't want to help me, go ahead and say so. I will understand. I don't want you to get involved, but I am slowly freezing and I am on the lam . . ."

"You mean you're running away from the hospital?"

"You could call it that."

"What kind of clothes?"

"Any kind at all. I haven't got a stitch."

She hesitated for a moment. Maybe she should ask the senator. But the senator wasn't home. He hadn't returned from the hospital and there was no telling when he would.

When she spoke again, she made her voice calm and hard. "Let me get this straight. You were the one who disappeared from the hospital, and without your clothes. And you say you aren't going back. You're on the lam, you say. You mean someone's hunting you?"

"For a while," he said, "the police were after me."

"But they aren't now?"

"No. Not for the moment. We gave them the slip."

"We?"

"I misspoke. I mean I got away from them."

She took a deep breath, committing herself. "Where are you?"

"I'm not absolutely sure. The city's changed since I knew it. I figure I'm out at the south end of the old Taft bridge."

"Stay there," she said. "Watch for my car. I'll slow down and be looking for you."

"Thanks . . ."

"Just a moment. Something occurred to me. You're calling from a public booth?"

"That's right."

"You need a coin to operate that kind of phone. Without any clothes, where did you get that coin?"

A sour grin split his face. "The coins drop into little boxes. I'm afraid I used a stone."

"You broke open the box to get a coin to use the phone?"

"Just a natural criminal," he said.

"I see. You'd better give me the number of the phone and stick close to it so I can call you if I can't find you—if you aren't where you think you are."

"Just a moment." He looked at the plate above the phone and read off the number. She found a pencil and copied the number on a newspaper margin.

"You realize," she said, "you're taking a chance on me. I've got you nailed to that phone and the number can be traced."

He made a wry face. "I realize that. But I've got to take the chance. You're the only one I have."

21

—This woman? Quester asked. She's a female, is she not?

—Yes, said Changer. Very much a female. Beautiful, I'd say.

—I grasp faintly at the connotation, Thinker said. The concept's new to me. A female is a being to whom one can demonstrate affection? The attraction, I take it, must be a mutual one. A female you can trust?

—Sometimes, said Changer. It depends on many things.

—I do not understand your attitude toward females, Quester grumbled. They are no more than continuators of the race. In the proper time and season . . .

—Your system, Thinker said, is inefficient and disgusting. If the need arises, I am my own continuator. The present question seems to be not the social or biological importance of this female, but is she someone we can trust?

—I don't know, said Changer. I think so. I've made a bet we can.

He crouched behind a clump of bushes, shivering. His teeth had a tendency to chatter. The wind, blowing from the north, had a touch of frost in it. He shifted his feet under him cautiously, trying to ease their soreness. He had stubbed his toes running in the dark and he'd stepped on something sharp and now his feet complained.

Out in the front of him stood the phone booth, the sign above it glowing dimly. Beyond the booth ran the street, practically deserted. Once in a while a ground car went thrumming along it, but always traveling fast. The bridge boomed hollowly as the cars passed over it.

Blake hunkered closer behind the bushes. Christ, he thought, what a situation! Squatting out here, naked and half frozen, waiting for a girl he'd seen only twice to bring him clothes and not entirely sure she would.

He grimaced, remembering the phone call. He had been compelled to crank up his courage to make it and he would not have blamed her if she'd not listened to him. But she had listened. Frightened, naturally, and perhaps somewhat suspicious, but who wouldn't be? A total stranger calling with a silly, if not embarrassing plea for help.

He had no claim on her. He knew that. And to make it even more ridiculous, this was the second time he'd been forced to call upon the senator's household for clothing to get him home. Although this time, he'd not be going home. The police would be watching and they'd nail him before he could get close.

He shivered and wrapped his arms about himself, in a futile attempt to conserve his body heat. From above him came a purring noise and he glanced quickly up. A house came slanting across the trees, losing altitude, perhaps heading for one of the downtown parking lots. Light shone from its windows and the sound of laughter and of music came to him. There were care-free, happy people up there while he crouched, shivering in the cold.

He watched the house until it disappeared, dropping east and lower.

And what did he do now? What did the three of them do now? Once he got the clothes, what would be his next move?

From what Elaine had said, he apparently was not as yet publicly identified as the man who had fled the hospital. But within hours the story would be out. Then his face would be staring from every printed page and would be on dimensino. In such a case he could not hope to escape being recognized. Either Thinker or Quester could take over the body, of course, and then there'd be no face to recognize, but either one of them would have to stay even more strictly out of sight than he. The climate was against them—too cold for Thinker and too hot for Quester, and there was the further complication that it was up to him to absorb and store up the energy that maintained and powered the body. There might be food that Quester could handle, but to determine it, research and testing would be needed. There were places, close to power sources, where Thinker could suck in energy, but they'd be hard to find and still stay undetected.

Would it be safe, he wondered, to try to contact Daniels? Thinking about it, he decided that it would be most unsafe. He knew the answer he would get—return to the hospital. And the hospital was a trap. There he would be subjected to endless interviews and further medical probing and, perhaps, a psychiatric treatment. He would not be in charge of himself. He would be politely guarded. He'd be a prisoner. And while man might have fabricated him, he fiercely told himself, he was not owned by man. He must remain himself.

And what about that self? Not man alone, of course, but man and two other creatures. Even if he wished, he never could escape those other minds that, with him, held joint ownership to this mass of matter which did service as their bodies. Now that he thought about it, he knew he did not wish to escape those minds. They were close to him, closer than anything else had ever been or could be. They were friends—well, perhaps not exactly friends, but collaborators existing in the common bonds of a single flesh. And even if they had not been friends and collaborators, there was yet another consideration he could not ignore. It had been through his agency that they were in this mess and, in light of that, he had no course but to stick with them to the end.

Would she come, he wondered, or would she turn her information over to the police or hospital? He could not bring himself to blame her, he told himself, if she did turn him in. How could she know that he was not mildly mad, or perhaps more mad than mildly? She might very well believe that she would be acting in his interest if she informed upon him.

Any moment now a police cruiser might come shrieking up and disgorge a freight of cops.

—Quester, Changer said, we may be in trouble. It's taking her too long.

—There are other ways, said Quester. If she fails us, we will find other ways.

—If the police show up, said Changer, we'll have to shift to you. I'd never be able to outrun them. I can't see too well in the dark and my feet are sore and . . .

—Any time you say, said Quester. I'll be ready. Just give me the word.

Down in the wooded valley a raccoon whickered. Blake shivered. Ten more minutes, he thought. I'll give her ten more minutes. If she doesn't show by that time, we'll get out of here. And he wondered how he was to know, without a watch, when ten minutes had gone past.

He crouched, miserable and shaken, lonely. An alien thing, he thought. Alien in a world of creatures of which he bore the shape. Was there any place, he asked himself, not only on this planet, but in the universe, for him? I'm human, he'd told Thinker; I insist on being human. But by what right did he insist?

—Steady, boy, said Quester. Steady. Steady. Steady.

Time wore on. The raccoon was silent. A bird twittered somewhere in the woods, wakened and disturbed by what prowling danger or what imagined threat?

A car came cruising slowly up the strip of paving. It

pulled up to the curb opposite the phone booth. The horn bleated softly.

Blake rose from behind his bush and waved his arms.

"Over here," he yelled.

The door of the car came open and Elaine stepped out. In the faint light of the weak bulb of the booth, he recognized her—the small oval of her face, the dark beauty of her hair. She carried a bundle in her hand.

She walked past the phone booth and moved toward the bush. Ten feet away she stopped.

"Here, catch," she said, and tossed the bundle.

Fingers stiff with cold, Blake unwrapped the bundle and got into the clothes. The sandals were stout, the robe of black wool and with a cowl attached.

Dressed, he stepped out and walked forward to join Elaine.

"Thanks," he said. "I was nearly frozen."

"I'm sorry that it took so long," she said. "I kept thinking of you hiding out here. But I had to get the stuff together."

"Stuff?"

"Things that you will need."

"I don't understand," he said.

"You said that you were on the run. You'll need more than clothes. Come on and get inside the car. I have the heater on. It is warm in there."

Blake drew back. "No," he told her. "Don't you understand? I can't let you involve yourself any further than you have. Not that I'm not grateful . . ."

"Nonsense," she said. "You're my good deed for the day."

He pulled the robe closer about himself.

"Look," she said, "you're cold. Get into the car."

He hesitated. He was cold and the car was warm.

"Come on," she said.

He went with her to the car, waited while she got in

and slid behind the wheel, then got in and closed the door. A hot blast struck his ankles.

She shifted a gear lever and the car moved forward.

"I can't stay parked," she said. "Someone would report me or investigate. So long as I keep moving, I am legal. Is there any place you would like to go?"

He shook his head. He hadn't even given thought to where he meant to go.

"Out of Washington, perhaps?"

"That is right," he said. Out of Washington was at least a start.

"Can you tell me about it, Andrew?"

"Not much," he said. "If I told you'd probably stop the car and throw me out."

She laughed. "Don't try to dramatize it, whatever it may be. I'm going to swing around and head west. Is that O.K. with you?"

"It's O.K.," he said. "There'll be places I can hide."

"How long—I mean how long do you think you'll have to stay in hiding?"

"I wouldn't know," he said.

"You know what I think? I don't believe you can hide at all. Someone will root you out. Your only chance is to keep moving around, not staying long at any place."

"You've thought a lot about it?"

"No. It just makes common sense. That robe I brought for you—one of Daddy's wool ones that he is so proud of—is the kind of get-up that roving students wear."

"Roving students?"

"Oh, I keep forgetting. You aren't caught up yet with all that's going on. They aren't really students. They're artistic bums. They wander around and some of them do paintings, some of them write books and some of them write poetry—you know, artistic stuff like that. There aren't many of them, but enough so they are recognized for what they are. And no one, of course, pays attention to them. You can pull up the hood of your robe and no one will get a good look at your face. Not that anyone would look."

"And you think I should be a roving student?"

She ignored the interruption. "I found an old knapsack for you. It's the kind of thing they use. Some pads of paper and some pencils and a book or two for you to read. You'd better take a look at them, so you know what they are. Whether you like it or not, you see, you will be a writer. First chance you get you scribble down a page or two. So that if anyone should question you, you will look authentic."

He huddled in the seat, soaking up the warmth. She had swung the car around to another street and was heading west. Great towering blocks of apartments rose against the sky.

"Reach into that compartment to your right," she said. "I suppose that you are hungry. I fixed up some sandwiches and a thermos full of coffee."

He reached his hand into the pocket and brought out a package, broke it open, took a sandwich.

"I was hungry," he said.

"I thought you'd be," she said.

The car went on. The apartment houses became fewer. Here and there were small villages with their gridworks of single houses.

"I could have wrangled a floater for you," she said. "Even a car, perhaps. But both of them carry licenses and would not be hard to trace. And, furthermore, no one pays much attention to a man trudging along on foot. You'll be safer that way."

"Elaine," he asked, "why go to so much bother for me? I didn't ask this much."

"I don't know," she said. "You've had such a damn poor time of it, I guess. Hauled in from space and then turned over to the hospital and pawed and scrutinized.

Put out to pasture for a while in that little village, then hauled in again."

"They were only doing what they could for me, of course."

"Yes, I know. But it couldn't have been pleasant. I don't blame you for running out when you had the chance."

They rode along in silence for a time. Blake ate the sandwiches and had some of the coffee.

"This wolf?" she asked suddenly. "What do you know about it? They said there was a wolf."

"So far as I know, there was no wolf," he said. He consoled himself that, technically, he was right. Quester was no wolf.

"The hospital was terribly upset," she said. "They phoned the senator to come down."

"Me or the wolf?" he asked.

"I don't know," she said. "He hadn't got back when I left."

They came to an intersection and she slowed the car, pulled off to the side of the road and stopped.

"This is as far as I can take you," she said. "I can't be too late getting back."

He opened the door, then hesitated. "Thanks," he said. "You've been a lot of help. I hope some day . . ."

"Just a minute there," she said. "Here's your knapsack. There is some money in it . . ."

"Now, wait . . ."

"No, you wait. You will need it. It's not too much, but it will carry you a ways. It's out of my allowance. You can pay me back some day."

He reached out and took the knapsack, looped the strap across his shoulder.

His voice was husky when he spoke. "Elaine—Elaine, I don't know what to say."

In the dimness of the car it seemed that she was closer

to him. Her shoulder touched his arm and he could smell the sweetness of her. Scarcely meaning to, he put out an arm and drew her close. He ducked down and kissed her. Her hand came up and cradled his head, her fingers cool and soft.

Then they were apart again and she was looking at him, with a sure and steady gaze.

"I wouldn't have helped you," she said, "if I hadn't liked you. I think that you're all right. I think you're doing nothing you need to be ashamed of."

He did not reply.

"Now, off with you," she said. "Out into the night. Later on, when you can, let me hear from you."

22

The eating place stood in the apex of a Y where the road forked in two directions. In the half-light of not-quite-dawn, the red sign that stood above its roof showed pink.

Blake limped a bit more rapidly. Here was a chance to soak up a little warmth while he rested, an opportunity to stow away some food. The sandwiches Elaine had provided him had carried him through the long night of walking, but now he was hungry again. With the coming of morning, he'd have to find a place where he could get some sleep and still be hidden—a haystack, perhaps. He wondered if there still were haystacks, or if even such simple things as haystacks had been swept away since he had known the earth.

The wind whipped wickedly out of the north and he pulled the cowl of the robe forward around his face. The strap of the knapsack was galling his shoulder and he tried to readjust it, to find an area of skin that had not been chafed, but it seemed that no such area remained.

He finally reached the diner and crossed the parking lot in front of it, climbed the short flight of stairs to the door. The place was empty. The counter gleamed from polishing, the chrome of the coffee urn shone brightly in the light of the lamps that marched across the ceiling.

"How are you?" asked the Diner. The voice was that of a brassy, wise-cracking waitress. "What will it be this morning?"

Blake looked around, seeing no one, then realized the

situation. Another robotic installation, like the flying houses.

He went across the floor and sat down on one of the stools.

"Cakes," he said, "and some bacon. And coffee."

He let the knapsack slip off his shoulder and lowered it to the floor beside the stool.

"Out early, aren't you?" asked the Diner. "Don't tell me you have walked all night."

"Not all night," said Blake. "Up early, that is all."

"Don't see many of you fellows any more," the Diner said. "What is your racket, friend?"

"I do a little writing," said Blake. "At least, I try to do it."

"Well," said the Diner, "at least you get to see some of the country. Me, I'm stuck here all the time. I never get to see anything at all. All I get is a lot of talk. Not," said the Diner, hastily, "that I dislike hearing talk. At least it's something to occupy my mind."

A spout poured a gob of batter on the griddle, moved along a traveling track to pour a second and a third, then snapped swiftly back to its original position. A metal arm mounted beside the coffee urn unfolded, extended itself and tripped a lever above the griddle. Three slices of bacon slid out and flopped upon the griddle. Deftly the arm descended and separated them, nudging them into a neat row.

"Want your coffee now?" asked the Diner.

"If you please," said Blake.

The metallic arm grasped a cup, held it under the faucet of the urn and raised it to activate the spout. Coffee poured out, the cup filled, the arm swung around and deposited it before Blake, then dipped down underneath the counter, came up with silverware, politely pushed the sugar dispenser closer to his reach.

"Cream?" the Diner asked.

"No, thanks," said Blake.

"Heard a good story the other day," the Diner said. "Fellow in here the other day sprung it on me. It seems that . . ."

Behind Blake, the door came open.

"No! No!" screamed the Diner. "You cut out of here. How often do I have to tell you never to come in when I got customers."

"I came in to see your customer," said a squeaky voice.

The sound of the voice spun Blake around.

A Brownie stood just inside the door, the bright, beady eyes glittering above the rodent snout, the high-domed skull flanked by the tasseled ears. Its trousers were striped green and pink.

"I feed it," wailed the Diner. "I put up with it. People say it's good luck to have one of them around, but this one never brings me anything but trouble. It is full of tricks. It is impertinent. It has no respect for me . . ."

"That's because you put on human airs," the Brownie said, "forgetting that you are not a human, but a stand-in for a human, taking away an honest job that a human might perform. I ask you why anyone should have respect for you?"

"No more handouts for you!" screamed the Diner. "No more sleeping in here when the nights are cold. Nothing more for you. I've had my fill of you."

The Brownie disregarded the tirade, came briskly across the floor. He stopped and made a formal bow to Blake.

"Good morning, honored sir. I hope I find you well."

"Very well," said Blake, amusement struggling with a deep sense of foreboding. "Would you have some breakfast with me?"

"Gladly," said the Brownie, leaping to the stool next to

Blake. He perched on it, with his feet dangling above the floor.

"Sir," he said, "I will have whatever you are having. It is most generous and courteous of you to ask me, for I hunger greatly."

"You heard my friend," said Blake, speaking to the Diner. "He will have what I am having."

"And you will pay for it?" asked the Diner.

"Most certainly I will."

The mechanical arm scooped up and flipped the baking cakes, moved them toward the griddle's front. The spout began spraying out new gobs of batter.

"It is a treat to eat a regular meal," said the Brownie, speaking confidentially to Blake. "Most people give me scraps. And while hunger cannot choose, the inner creature sometimes craves more consideration."

"Don't let him take you in," the Diner cautioned Blake. "Buy him this breakfast, if you must, but then shake free of him. Don't let him fasten onto you, or he will suck you dry."

"Machines," the Brownie said, "have no sensibilities. They are ignorant of the finer instincts. They are callous to the suffering of the very ones they are meant to serve. And they have no souls."

"Neither have you, you heathen alien," raged the Diner. "You are a chiseler and a moocher and you are a parasite. You use humankind most unmercifully and you have no gratitude and you don't know when to stop."

The Brownie slanted his rodent eyes at Blake and lifted both of his hands, palms upward, in a hopeless gesture.

"Well, you don't," the Diner said, aggrieved. "There is solemn truth in every word I said."

The arm scooped up the first three cakes, put them on a plate, ranged the bacon alongside them, punched a button and caught, with great dexterity, the three pats of butter ejected from a chute. The arm set the plate in front of Blake, darted down underneath the counter and came up with a jug of syrup.

The Brownie's nose twitched with pleasure. "They smell delicious," he said.

"No snitching!" screamed the Diner. "You wait till yours are done."

From far off came a faint moaning bleat.

The Brownie stiffened, its ears stretched up and flaring. The moaning came again.

"It's another one of them!" the Diner yelled. "They are supposed to warn us well ahead of time, not come sneaking up on us like this. And you, you no-good chiseler, are supposed to be out there, listening for the first sign of them. That's what I feed you for."

"It's way too soon for another one," the Brownie said. "There shouldn't be another one through until late this evening. They are supposed to spread themselves out, to use different roads so one road doesn't have to put up with them all the time."

The moaning came again, louder and closer—a lonesome, wailing sound trailing off the hills.

"What is it?" asked Blake.

"It's a cruiser," the Brownie told him, "One of these big sea-going freighters. It has a load of something that it's carried all the way from Europe, maybe from Africa, and it came ashore an hour or so ago and is coming up the road."

"You mean it doesn't stop when it reaches shore?"

"Why should it?" asked the Brownie. "It travels on the same principle as the ground cars, on a cushioned jet stream. It can travel on either land or water. It comes up to shore and never hesitates—just goes booming down a road."

Metal screeched and thudded on metal. Blake saw that great steel shutters were creeping across the outside of the windows. Clamps swivelled out of the wall and moved against the door, snugging it tight.

The moaning filled the room now and far off there was a terrible howling, as if a gigantic storm moved across the land.

"All battened down!" The Diner screamed to be heard above the noise. "You guys better hit the floor. This sounds like a big one."

The building was shaking and the noise was a numbing cataract that poured from all directions to fill the room to bursting.

The Brownie had nipped beneath the stool and was hanging tightly, both arms wrapped about the metal standard on which the stool was mounted. His mouth was open and it was evident that he was yelling at Blake, but his voice was engulfed and drowned out by the howling that was coming up the road.

Blake threw himself off the stool and hugged the floor. He tried to hook his fingers into the floor, but the floor covering was a hard, smooth plastic and he could get no grip on it.

The diner seemed to buck and the howling of the cruiser was almost unendurable. Blake felt himself sliding on the floor.

Then the howling tapered off and died away, became a faint, long-drawn and distorted moaning.

Blake picked himself off the floor.

A lake of coffee lay upon the counter where his cup had been and there was no sign of the cup. The plate on which the cakes and bacon had rested was on the floor, smashed and scattered. The cakes lay limply on the stool. The cakes meant for the Brownie still were on the griddle, but were smoking and had turned black around the edges.

"I'll start over," said the Diner.

The arm reached out and snatched up a spatula,

scraped the burned cakes off the griddle, flipped them into a garbage can underneath the burner.

Blake looked over the counter and saw that the space behind it was littered with broken crockery.

"Yeah, look at it!" the Diner screeched. "There ought to be a law. I'll notify the boss and he'll slap a claim against that outfit and he'll see they pay—he always has so far. You guys might want to file claims as well. Allege mental agony or something. I got claim forms if you want to do it."

Blake shook his head. "What about motorists. What if you met that thing on the road?"

"You saw those bunkers along the road, ten feet high or so, with exit lanes leading up to them?"

"Yes, I did," said Blake.

"The cruiser has to sound its horn as soon as it leaves water and starts traveling on land. It has to keep on sounding it all the time it's traveling. You hear that siren and you head for the nearest bunker and you duck behind it."

The spigot traveled deliberately along its track, pouring out the batter.

"How come, mister," asked the Diner, "you didn't know about the cruisers and the bunkers? You come from the backwoods, maybe?"

"It's none of your business," said the Brownie, speaking for Blake. "Just get on with our breakfast."

23

"I'll walk you a piece down the road," said the Brownie when they left the diner.

The morning sun was topping the horizon behind them and their elongated shadows bobbed along the road in front of them. The paving, Blake noted, was broken and eroded.

"They don't keep up the roads," he said, "the way I remember them."

"No need to," said the Brownie. "No wheels. No need of a smooth surface since there isn't any contact. The cars all ride on cushions of air. They only need roads as designation strips and to keep the traffic out of people's hair. Now, when they lay out a new road, they just set out a double row of stakes, to show the drivers the location of the highway."

They jogged along, not hurrying. A flock of blackbirds rose in a blue of flashing wings out of a marshy swale off to the left.

"Flocking up," the Brownie said. "They'll be leaving soon. Cheeky things, the blackbirds. Not like larks or robins."

"You know about these wild things?"

"We live with them," the Brownie said. "We get to understand them. Some we get so we can almost talk with them. Not birds, though. Birds and fish are stupid. But raccoons and foxes, muskrats and mink—they are all real people."

"You live out in the woods, I understand."

"In the woods and fields. We conform to ecology. We take things as we find them. We adapt to circumstances. We are blood brothers to all life. No quarrels with anyone."

Blake tried to remember what Daniels had told him. A strange sort of little people who had taken a liking to the Earth, not because of the dominant life form that inhabited it, but because of the planet itself. Perhaps, Blake thought, because they found in the non-dominant residents, in the few remaining wild denizens of the woods and fields the sort of simple associations that they liked. Insisting on living their own way of life to go their independent way, and yet beggars and moochers, attaching themselves in a slipshod alliance with anyone who would provide whatever simple needs they had.

"I met another of your people a few days ago," said Blake. "You'll pardon me, but I can't be sure. Could you . . ."

"Oh, no," the Brownie said. "That was another one of us. He was the one who spotted you."

"Spotted me?"

"Oh, yes, indeed. As one who would bear watching. He said that there was more than one of you and that you were in trouble. He sent out word we should, any one of us who could, keep an eye on you."

"Apparently you've been doing a good job of it. It didn't take you long to pick me up."

"When we set out to accomplish something," the Brownie said, with pride, "we can be most efficient."

"And I? Where do I fit in?"

"I am not sure exactly," said the Brownie. "We are to keep an eye on you. You only need to know we're watching. You can count on us."

"I thank you," Blake told him. "I thank you very much."

And that was all he needed, he told himself—to have these crazy little creatures keeping tabs on him.

They walked along in silence for a time and then Blake asked: "He told you, this one that I met, to keep an eye on me . . ."

"Not just me alone . . ."

"I know that," said Blake. "He told all of you. Would you mind explaining how he told the rest of you? Or maybe it's a stupid question. There are mail and telephones."

The Brownie made a clucking sound of immense disgust. "We wouldn't be caught dead," he said, "using such contrivances. It would be against our principles and there really is no need to use them. We just pass the word along."

"You mean you are telepathic."

"Well, to tell you the honest truth, I don't know if we are or not. We can't transmit words, if that is what you mean. But we have a oneness. It gets a bit hard to explain."

"I would imagine so," said Blake. "A sort of tribal psychic grapevine."

"You don't make any sense to me," the Brownie said, "but if you want to think of it that way, I guess it does no harm."

"I suppose," said Blake, "there are a lot of people that you keep an eye on."

It would be just like them, he told himself, a bunch of little busybodies very much concerned with other people's lives.

"There are no others," said the Brownie. "Not at the moment, anyhow. He told us there were more than one of you and . . ."

"What has that got to do with it?"

"Why, bless you," said the Brownie, "that's the whole of it. How often does one find a creature there is more than one of? Would you mind telling me, I wonder, just how many . . ."

"There are three of me," said Blake.

The Brownie jigged in triumph. "I knew there were," he crowed. "I made a bet with myself that there were three of you. One of you is warm and shaggy, but with a terrible temper. Can you tell me this is so?"

"Yes," said Blake, "I would suppose it is."

"But the other one of you," the Brownie said, "baffles me entirely."

"Welcome to the club," said Blake. "He baffles me as well."

24

When he topped the long, steep hill, Blake saw it in the valley, where the land dipped down and ran level for a mile or so, then climbed another hill. It rested on the level of the valley floor and it seemed to fill half the level space—a great, black bulging structure that looked amazingly like a monstrous bug, humped in its middle and blunted at both ends.

Blake stopped at the sight of it. He had never seen a cruiser, but there could be no doubt that the thing squatting at the bottom of the hill was the cruiser which had shaken up the diner.

Cars went whipping past Blake, the gush of wind from their humming jets beating at him.

The Brownie had left him an hour before and since that time he had trudged along, looking for someplace where he might hide away and sleep. But stretching on either side the road was nothing but fields, stripped by the harvest, now lying in their autumn garb of brown and gold. No habitations were located near the road, all of them sitting back from it half a mile or so. Blake wondered if the use of this highway by the cruisers and probably other large conveyances as well might have dictated the position of the homesteads, or if there were some other reason for their off-the-road location.

Far off to the southwest loomed a small group of shimmering towers—perhaps a complex of high-rise apartments, still within easy distance of Washington, but giving their occupants the advantages of a rural life.

Blake, staying well out on the shoulder of the road, went down the hill and finally reached the cruiser. It had pulled off to one side of the highway and had settled down, roosting on stubby, peg-like legs that held it six feet or so above the ground. Close up, it was even larger than it had appeared at a distance, rearing twenty feet or more above Blake's head.

At its forward end a man sat, leaning against the flight of steps that led up to the cab. He sat flat, with his legs stuck out in front of him and he wore a greasy engineer's cap pulled down almost to his eyes. His tunic was pulled up and bunched about his middle.

Blake stopped and stood looking down at him.

"Good morning, friend," said Blake. "It looks to me that you are in trouble."

"Greetings to you, Brother," said the man, taking in Blake's black robe and knapsack. "You are seeing right. Burned out a jet and she began to whipsaw me. Lucky that I didn't pile it up."

He spat derisively in the dust. "Now we have to sit and wait. I radioed in for a new jet component and a repair crew and they take their time, of course."

"You said we."

"There are three of us," said the engineer. "Two others are up there, sacking out."

He jerked his thumb upward toward the small living quarters installed behind the cab.

"We were on schedule, too," he said. "That's the tough part of it. Made a good crossing—calm seas and we hit no coastal fog. But now we'll be hours late when we hit Chicago. There's overtime, of course, but who the hell wants any overtime."

"You're headed for Chicago?"

"Yeah. This time. Always different places. Never the same place twice."

He reached up and pulled at the beak of his cap.

"I keep thinking of Mary and the kids," he said.

"Your family? Surely you can get in touch with them, let them know what happened."

"Tried to. But they aren't home. Finally asked the operator to get someone to go out and tell them I wouldn't be along. Not right away, at least. You see, whenever I take this road, they know when I'll be coming and they go down to the road and stand there and wait and wave at me as I go through. The kids get an awful kick out of it, seeing their old man driving this monster."

"You must live near here," said Blake.

"Little town," said the engineer. "Little backwater place a hundred miles or so from here. Old town, stuck out of the way. Just the way it was two hundred years ago. Oh, they put a new front on one of the buildings down on Main street every now and then, or someone remodels a house, but mostly the town just sits there, the way it always was. None of these big apartment complexes they are building everywhere. Nothing new at all. Good place to live. Easy-going place. No one doing any pushing. No Chamber of Commerce. No one lathering to get rich. Anyone who wants to get rich or get ahead or anything like that simply doesn't stay there. Lots of fishing, some hunting. Some horseshoe pitching."

He glanced up at Blake. "I guess you get the picture."

Blake nodded.

"Good place to raise kids," said the engineer.

He picked up a dried weed stalk off the ground, poked gently at the earth with it.

"Town by the name of Willow Grove," he said. "You ever hear of it?"

"No," said Blake, "I don't think I ever . . ."

But that was not correct, he realized suddenly. He had heard of it! That message on the P.G. that had been waiting for him when the guard had brought him home from the senator's house had mentioned Willow Grove.

"You have heard of it, then," said the engineer.

"I guess I have," said Blake. "Someone mentioned it to me."

"A good place to live," said the man.

What had that message said? Contact someone in the town of Willow Grove and he'd learn something to his interest. And there had been the name of the man he should contact. What was that name again? Blake sought for it frantically, winnowing through his mind, but it wasn't there.

"I must be getting on," he said. "I hope the service crew shows up."

The man spat in disgust. "Oh, they'll be along all right. When they are good and ready."

Blake trudged on, facing the long hill which rose above the valley. At the top of the hill, he saw, were trees, a humped line of autumn color ranging above the high horizon line, a break at last in the brown and yellow fields. Perhaps somewhere among those trees he could find a place where he could get some sleep.

Thinking back, Blake tried to call up the fantasy of the night, but there was still about it all an air of unreality. It was almost as if it were a series of incidents which had happened, not to him, but to someone else.

The hunt for him still was on, of course, but momentarily he must have slipped the clutches of authority. By now, perhaps, Daniels would have figured out what must have happened and now they'd be looking, not for a wolf alone, but for him as well.

He reached the top of the hill and ahead of him, down the slope, he saw the trees, not just a little grove of trees, but a woods that covered the greater part of the steep hillside on either side of the road. Below, where the valley leveled out, were fields, but beyond the valley the farther slope also was clothed with trees. Here, he realized, the folded hills began to rise too steeply for cultivation and that this alternating of cultivated valleys and wooded hills might be a pattern that would go on for miles.

He went down the hill and at the edge of the woods his eyes caught a furtive movement. Alerted and puzzled, he watched for it again. It could have been, he knew, a bird hopping from one branch to another in a low-growing shrub, or, perhaps, an animal. But the woods now was quiet, except for a slight stirring of the many-colored leaves by the whisper of a lazy wind.

He came opposite the edge of the woods and something hissed at him.

He stopped, half frightened, and shifted around to stare into the underbrush beneath the trees.

"Over here!" whispered a high and squeaky voice, and it was then, guided by the voice, that he saw the Brownie—brown fur and dark green trousers— camouflaged within the forest growth.

Another one of them, he thought. Good God, another one of them and this time he had no food to offer.

He stepped quickly off the shoulder of the road, across the ditch, and into the edge of the woods. The Brownie remained only a dim outline, blending with the woods, until he was quite close to him.

"I've been watching for you," said the Brownie. "I understand you're tired and might want a place to rest."

"That is true," said Blake. "There was nothing, until now, but fields."

"You, then," the Brownie said, "are welcome to my home. If you do not object to sharing it with an unfortunate creature which I offered my protection."

"Not at all," said Blake. "This other creature?"

"A raccoon," said the Brownie, "chased most pitilessly by a pack of hounds and cornered and mauled considerably, but managing to escape. In these hills, you must understand, there is a popular human sport, which you may have heard of, known as coon hunting."

"Yes," said Blake, "I have heard of it."

But he knew, well enough, that he had not remembered it until the Brownie spoke of it.

Once again, he thought, a phrase had triggered another memory, unsuspected until this moment, and another piece of his human background had fallen smoothly into place. He became aware of that memory, sharply aware of it—the lantern-lighted night, standing on a hilltop, with a gun clutched in one hand, waiting for the dogs to pick up the trail and then, suddenly, the far-off bugling of a hound that had struck a scent. And in a moment other dogs joining in until the hill and valley rang with baying. He smelled again the sweet, peculiar odor of frosted, fallen leaves, saw once again the bare branches of the trees against the risen moon, and the thrill of following the chase as the hounds ranged up the hill. Then the headlong plunge down the slope, guided only by the feeble lantern light, hurrying to close in with the hounds and not be left behind.

"I have tried to explain to the raccoon," the Brownie said, "that if you came you would be a friend. I am not too sure, however, that he understood. He is not too bright an animal and he is, as you can well imagine, still suffering a trauma."

"I will try not to alarm him," Blake assured the Brownie. "I will make no sudden moves. Will there be room for the both of us?"

"Oh, most assuredly," the Brownie said. "My home is a hollow tree. There is a great deal of room in it."

Good Lord, thought Blake, could this be really happening—standing out here in the woods, talking to a thing that should be snared inside a children's book, being invited to den up in a hollow tree and share it with a coon.

And from where had come the memory of the coon hunt? Had he ever, actually, been on such a hunt? It seemed impossible. For he knew what he was—a chemically-processed human, and processed for one purpose and for one purpose only, and it seemed unlikely, in view of that, he'd ever hunted coon.

"If you will follow me," the Brownie said, "I will lead you to the tree."

Blake followed the Brownie and it seemed to him that he had stepped into a mad painter's fairyland. Jewel-like leaves of every shade of gold and red hung on all the undergrowth, the saplings, the shrubby bushes, the very woodland plants—matching in finer detail and more delicate and brighter colors the riot of autumn pigments in the overhanging trees. And once again the memory of another place, or perhaps many other places, such as this, came back again to him. Memories with no detail as to time or place, but breath-catching in the remembered beauty of another woods on another day, caught in that instant of time when the autumn hues were at their brightest and their best, before the first hint of deterioration had touched them, at that exact moment before they would begin to fade.

They followed a faint trail, so faint that few eyes could have picked it out.

"It is pretty in here," said the Brownie. "I like autumn best of all. I understand that on the old home planet there was no such thing as autumn."

"You still know about your planet?"

"Of course," the Brownie said. "The old stories are passed on. It is still our heritage. In time, I would imagine, we will forget about it, for Earth then will be our planet. But as yet, we must maintain a solid grip on the both of them."

They came to a mammoth tree, a mighty oak eight feet or more across its trunk, gnarled and misshapen, twisted, with the heavy scales of lichen colonies turning its bark into brown and silver. Around its base grew heavy ranks of ferns. The Brownie pulled the ferns apart.

"In here," he told Blake. "I apologize, but you must get down on your hands and knees and crawl. It is not a place that was designed for humans."

Blake got down and crawled. The ferns rubbed across his face and brushed his neck and then he was in a soft, cool darkness that smelled of ancient wood. From someplace up above a little light filtered down to break up the darkness.

He twisted carefully around and sat down cautiously.

"In a little time," the Brownie said, standing at his elbow, "your eyes will become accustomed to the gloom and you can see again."

"I can see a little now," said Blake. "There is some light."

"From knotholes higher up the trunk," the Brownie told him. "The tree is dying of old age. It is nothing but a shell. Once, long ago, it was scarred by a forest fire and that gave the rot a chance to work. But unless it is shaken by too great a wind, it will last for many years. And in the meantime it serves as a home for us, and higher up, there is a home for a family of squirrels. And the nests of many birds, although by now most of the birds have left. Through the years this tree has been home to many things. Living in it, there is a feeling of belonging."

His eyes had become somewhat adjusted to the darkness and now Blake could see the inside of the tree. The inner surface was fairly smooth; all loose rot apparently had been removed. The hollow core rose like a shaft above his head and far up this tunnel, Blake could see small areas of brightness where knotholes let in the light.

"You will be undisturbed," the Brownie said. "There are two others of us. I might suppose, in the human terminology, they would be described as wives. But they are rather shy of humans. And there are some children, too."

"I'm sorry," Blake said. "I would not think . . ."

"No need of sorrow," said the Brownie. "The wives will turn their time to much good use in the gathering of roots and nuts and the children never stay here anyhow. They have so many woodlands friends that they spend all their time with them."

Blake looked about the tree. There was nothing in it.

"No furniture," the Brownie told him, quietly. "No material possessions. We have never needed them; we do not need them now. We have some food—caches of nuts and corn and grain and roots—stored against the winter, but that is all we have. You will, I hope, think none the less of us for this improvidence."

Blake shook his head, half in answer, half in bewilderment.

Something stirred quietly in a darkened angle of the tree-house and Blake turned his head. A masked, furry face peered out at him, eyes shining in the darkness.

"Our other friend," the Brownie said. "He does not seem to be afraid of you."

"I shall do nothing to harm him," said Blake, a little stiffly.

"You are hungry?" asked the Brownie. "We have . . ."

"No, thanks," said Blake. "I ate this morning, with a compatriot of yours."

The Brownie nodded, sagely. "He told me you were coming. That's why I waited for you. He could not offer you a place to sleep; he has nothing but a burrow, quite too small for humans."

The Brownie turned to go.

"I don't quite know," said Blake, "how I am to thank you."

"You have already thanked us," the Brownie said.

"You have accepted us and accepted aid from us. And that is most important, I assure you, for ordinarily it is we who seek help from humans. To pay back a fraction of that help is very precious to us."

Blake looked around at the raccoon. It still was watching him with its fire-bright eyes. When he looked back, the Brownie was gone.

Blake reached out and pulled his knapsack to him, rummaged in its contents. A thin and compact blanket, unlike anything he had ever seen, with a strange metallic luster; a knife in a sheath; a folding axe; a small kit of cooking utensils; a lighter and a can of fluid; a folded map; a flashlight; a——.

A map!

He picked it up and unfolded it, used the flashlight to light it, leaning close to make out the place names.

Willow Grove, a hundred miles or so away, the engineer had said. And there it was, the place that he was going. Finally, he thought, a destination in this world and situation where there had seemed to be no destinations. A place upon a map and a person, with an unremembered name, who had information that might be of interest to him.

He laid the blanket to one side and put the rest of the items back into the knapsack.

The raccoon, he saw, had crept a little closer, its curiosity apparently aroused by the things he had taken from the knapsack.

Blake moved over close to the wall, unfolded the blanket and pulled it over his body, tucked it in and lay down. The blanket seemed to cling to him, as if his body were a magnet, and for all its thinness there was warmth in it. The floor was soft and there were no lumps in it. Blake picked up a handful of the substance that composed it, and let it run slowly through his fingers. Tiny fragments of rotted wood, he saw, fragments that for years had fallen down from the tunnel of the hollowed trunk.

He closed his eyes and sleep crept in on him. His consciousness seemed to sink into a pit and there was something in the pit—two other selves that caught and held him and surrounded him so that he became one with them. Like a coming home, like a meeting with old friends not seen for much too long. There were no words and no words were needed. There was a welcome and an understanding and a seeming oneness and he was no longer Andrew Blake, and was not even human, but a being for which there was no name, and something that measured greater than either Andrew Blake or human.

But through the oneness and the comfort and the welcome an intruding thought stole out to nag him. He struggled and was let go and became himself again, an identity once more—not Andrew Blake, but Changer.

—Quester, when we awake, it will be colder then. Could you take over for the night? You can travel faster and you can sense your way through the darkness and . . .

—I'll take over. But there are your clothes and knapsack and you'll be naked once again and . . .

—You can carry them. You have arms and hands, remember? You are all the time forgetting that you have your arms.

—All right! said Quester. All right! All right! All right!

—Willow Grove, said Changer.

—Yes, I know, said Quester. We read the map with you.

The sleep began closing in again, but something touched his arm and he let his eyes come open.

The raccoon, he saw, had crept across the space between them and now lay close against him.

He lifted a corner of the blanket and tucked it about the furry body and then he went to sleep.

25

Changer had said that it would be cooler, and it was cooler, but still too warm for running, too warm for making any time. But, as Quester reached the ridgetop, the wind knifing from the north had a welcome bite to it.

He stopped and stood there, on the flinty ground, exposed to the wind, for here, for some reason of geology, the trees did not intrude, but stopped short of the crest, a somewhat unusual circumstance, since most of the hills were completely covered by the hardwood forest.

The skies were clear and there were stars this night, although it seemed to Quester not as many stars as could be seen from his native planet. And here, on this high piece of ground, he thought, one could stand and snare pictures from the stars, although now he knew from Thinker that they were not pictures only, but the kaleidoscopic impressions of other races and other cultures and that they supplied the raw, bare-bones data from which the truth of the universe might someday be deduced.

He shivered, thinking of it—thinking of how his mind and senses could reach across the light-years to harvest the fruits of other minds and senses. He shivered, but he knew even as he did that Thinker would not shiver, even had Thinker been so built, with muscle and with nerves, so that he could shiver. For there was nothing, absolutely nothing, that could astonish Thinker; to him there was no mystic quality in the universe or life, but rather a mass of fact and data, of principle and method, which could be fed into his mind and be utilized by his faculty for logic.

But for me, thought Quester, for me it all is mystic. To me there is no need of reason, no compulsion reaching out for logic, no cold, no intensive drive to burrow to the heart of fact.

He stood on the flinty ridge, his tail drooping almost to the ground, his grizzled muzzle lifted to the sharp edge of the wind. For him it was enough, he thought, that the universe was filled with wonder and with beauty and he had never asked for more—and he knew now that it was his fervent hope that nothing ever would occur to blunt that wonder and the beauty.

Or had that process of blunting already taken place? Had he placed himself in a position (or been placed in a position) where he would find himself with a greater scope than ever to seek out new wonders and fresh mysteries, but with the wonder and the beauty watered down by the knowledge that he was providing material for Thinker to work out the logic?

He tried to test the thought, but as yet the mysticism and the wonder still were his. Here, on this windswept ridge, with the stars shining in the sky above, with the wind blowing through the woods below him, and the woods talking to the dark, with the strange, alien smells and the other-worldly vibrations that shivered in the air, there still was room for wonder that ran like a chill along his nerves.

The space between him and the next hilltop seemed clear of any threat. Far off to the left ribbons of moving lights marked the passing of the cars along the road that cut across the hills. In the valley were habitations, betrayed by beams of light and by the vibrations that came streaming out from them—vibrations, radiations (whatever one might call them) of human life itself and of that strange force the humans called electricity.

There were birds roosting in the trees and some sort of

larger animal (although smaller than himself) sneaked through the underbrush to the right of him, mice huddled in their nests, a woodchuck in his den—and uncounted hordes of little burrowers and tiny scavengers moving in the soil and its mulch of rotting leaves. But these he screened out of his consciousness, for at the moment they were no concern of his.

He went quietly down the hill, through the woods, marking every tree and bush along his path, cataloguing and evaluating all the larger creatures, alert for any danger, fearing only that he might meet a danger he would not recognize.

The trees came to an end and the fields were ahead of him—the fields and roads and houses—and here again he hesitated to search out the land ahead.

A human was walking down by the creek with his dog and a car was moving slowly up a private road that ran to a house across the creek, a herd of cows were sleeping in a field, but except for these, the valley seemed clear except for mice and gophers and other smaller residents.

He started across the valley at a trot, then broke into an easy, rocking lope that ate up the ground. He reached the slope of the next high hill and went swarming over it and down the other side.

He hugged the knapsack underneath his left arm and the sack was bulky because it held Changer's clothes as well as all the other items. It was a bother, for it lent him a lop-sided balance for which he must compensate and he must forever be on guard against its being snagged by a bush or branch.

He halted for a moment, dropped the knapsack to the ground and retracted his left arm. Relieved of its burden, the arm snuggled wearily into the pocket in his shoulder. He extruded his right arm and picked up the sack, tucked it underneath the arm and resumed his traveling. Perhaps, he told himself, he should shift the burden oftener, from one arm to the other. It might be easier if he did.

He crossed the valley, went up the next long hill, stopped at its crest to rest a moment before going on.

Willow Grove, Changer had said. A hundred miles. He could be there by dawn if he kept on as he had been going. And what might await the three of them when they reached Willow Grove? Willow was a tree and grove was a group of trees, and it was strange how humans named certain geographic points. There was little logic to it, for a willow grove could die and disappear and then the placename would have no significance.

Impermanent, he thought. But then the humans, themselves, as a race, were impermanent. Their continual changing of their lives, this thing that they called progress, made for impermanence. There was something to be said, he thought, for forging the sort of life a race might wish to live, to set up some basic values, and then be satisfied.

He took a step down the hill, then stopped, tensed and listening.

The sound came again—a faint, far bugling.

A dog, he told himself. A dog that had struck a trail.

He went swiftly, but cautiously, down the hill, sensing ahead and on either side. At the edge of the wood, he stopped to survey the stretch of level valley that lay ahead of him. There was nothing there that was a matter of concern, and he trotted out into the valley, came to a fence and leaped in and then went on.

For the first time, he felt a twinge of fatigue. Despite the relative coolness of the night, he was unused to the heat of Earth. He had been pushing hard, trying to cover as much ground as possible, to reach Willow Grove by morning. He'd have to take it easier for a while, hope to get his second wind. He must pace himself.

He crossed the valley at a trot, not breaking into a

lope, reached the opposite slope and climbed it slowly.
On the crest, he told himself, he would sit down and rest
a while and by the time he started out again, he probably
could resume his former pace.

Halfway up the slope he heard the baying once again
and it seemed closer now and louder. It was whipped by
the wind, however, and he could not be sure exactly how
far away it was, or in what direction.

On the crest he halted and sat down. The moon was
rising and the trees in which he sat threw long shadows
out across a tiny meadow that lay on the steep hillside.

The baying definitely was closer now and there were
more dogs than one. He tried to count them. There were
four at least, perhaps five or six.

Coon-hunting, perhaps. The Brownie had said something about certain humans using dogs to chase raccoons,
calling it a sport. But there was, of course, no sport in it.
To think of anything like that as a sport called for a
peculiar perversion—although, come to think of it, the
humans seemed perverted in more ways than one. Honest
war was something else, of course, but this was neither
war nor honest.

The baying was coming up the slope behind him and
coming fast. There was now a frantic, slobbering sound in
the yelping of the dogs. They were hot upon the trail and
coming fast.

Hot upon the trail!

Quester leaped to his feet and swung about, thrusting
the sensor cone down the slope behind him. And there
they were—driving up the hill, noses no longer to the
ground, but lifted high to catch the scent that they had
followed.

The realization struck him now—the thing he should
have guessed, even back on the other hill when he first
had heard the baying. The dogs were following no coon.
They had struck on bigger game.

A thrill of horror shot through him and he spun about, to go plunging down the hill. Behind him, as the dog pack topped the hill, the wild song of the chase, no longer baffled by the rising slope of ground, rang out bugle-clear.

Quester flattened low against the ground, his legs a blur of speed, his tail floating out behind him. He reached the valley and crossed it and charged up the slope of the farther hill. He had gained distance on the dogs, but once again he felt the tiredness draining the strength out of his body and he knew the final outcome—he could outrun his pursuers in frantic bursts of speed, but in the end he'd lose, be overhauled when fatigue built up and slowed him down. Perhaps, he thought, the wiser thing would be to choose his ground and turn to wait for them. But there were too many of them. Two or three—he was sure he could handle two or three. But there were more than three. He could throw away the knapsack and, relieved of its weight and the unbalancing effect of it, he could run the faster. But the advantage would be slight and he had promised Changer he'd hang onto it. Changer would be annoyed if he abandoned it. Changer already was annoyed with him for occasionally forgetting that he had arms and hands.

It was strange, he thought, that the dogs should trail him. As an alien to this planet, he must be different than anything the dogs had ever known, must leave a different kind of trail, must have a different scent. But the difference (if there were a difference) seemed to instill no fear in them, had seemed to do no more than rouse them to a higher hunting frenzy. Perhaps, he told himself, he was not so much unlike the creatures of this planet as he would have thought.

He went on, but at a slower pace, settling into a determined lope and seeming to hold his own, but he was tiring much too fast. Before too long he'd be forced to exert himself to keep ahead and when that happened, he knew the end would be in sight.

He could, of course, call on Changer to take over. Perhaps the dogs would break off their trailing if the trail turned into a human trail, or even if they did continue to follow it, would not attack a man. But he shrank from doing this. He should, he told himself, hold up his end. He found in himself a stubborn pride that would not let him call on Changer.

He topped the rise and below him lay the valley and in the valley a house with one lighted window shining. And in his mind a plan began to form.

Not Changer, but Thinker. That might turn the trick.

—Thinker, you can extract energy from a house?

—Yes, of course. I did it once before.

—From outside the house?

—If I am close enough.

—All right, then. When I get . . .

—Carry on, said Thinker. I know what's in your mind.

Quester trotted down the hill, let the dogs close in, increased his speed when he struck the valley, heading for the house. The baying tapered off as the dogs, with the quarry now in sight, used every ounce of strength, every gasp of breath, to finally close upon it.

Quester glanced around and saw them, bunched together—terrible, striving shadows in the moonlight and across the space between them came an anxious whimpering, the excited sobbing of animals that closed in for the kill.

And then, suddenly, the baying burst out again, the cry of blood that rang across the sky and bounced against the hills.

The house now was only a little distance off and suddenly, as the baying bellowed in the night, more lights came on and from a pole outside the house a floodlight burst into blinding brilliance. Someone inside, apparently, had been aroused by the bloodthirsty clamor of the hounds.

A low picket fence separated the house from the field and Quester cleared the fence, landing in the full glare of the floodlight. With a sudden dash, he reached the house and huddled close against it.

—Now, he yelled to Thinker. Now!

26

It was cold, a biting, deadening cold, like a physical blow that staggered the body and the mind.

The satellite of the planet hung above a ragged line of uplifted vegetation and the land was sterile and dry, while across the construction the humans called a fence leaped the raging creatures that were designated dogs.

But somewhere close was a bank of energy and Thinker grabbed at it—in need, in desperation, almost in a panic. Grabbed at it and took it, more than he had need of, far more than he had need of. The house went dark and on the pole the floodlight flickered and went out.

The cold was gone and his body fell into the pyramidal form and it glowed. The data was there once again, as it had been before, sharper, more concise than it had ever been before, ranged in ranks and files, waiting to be used. Inside his mind the logic process was clean and bright and sharp and it had been far too long since he had made use of it.

—Thinker, Quester yelled. Cut it out! The dogs! The dogs! The dogs!

And that was right, of course. He had known about the dogs and of Quester's plan and the plan was working.

The dogs were swerving, digging in their claws to halt their headlong rush, whimpering and yelping in sudden abject fright at this apparition which had replaced the wolf they had been chasing.

There was too much energy, Thinker realized with a prick of fear. Far too much—more than he could handle.

He got rid of it.

He flared.

Crackling lightning flashed and the valley for a moment was lit up by the flare. The paint on the house curled and blackened, peeled.

The dogs, leaping back across the fence, howled as the lightning speared out at them. They fled, their tails tucked tight, their blistered rumps still smoking.

27

Willow Grove, Blake told himself, was a town that he had known sometime in the past. Which was impossible, of course. Perhaps a place very like a place that he might have read of, or at some time had seen a picture of, but he never had been here.

And yet, as he stood on the street corner in the early morning light, old memories kept nagging at him and a pattern in his mind kept matching the things that he was seeing—the way the steps up to the bank ran kitty-cornered off the sidewalk, and the massive elm trees that grew around the little park at the far end of the street. There would be, he knew, a statue in the park, standing in the center of a fountain that was dry more often than it ran, and an ancient cannon mounted on its massive wheels, its barrel bespecked by pigeon dirt.

Not always matching, but also noting differences. A hobby shop and jewelry store occupied the building where the garden store had been and a new front had been imposed upon the barber shop, which still was a barber shop, and over all of it, over the entire street and town, lay an oldness that had not been there when he last had seen it.

Last had seen it!

Could he, he wondered, have ever seen this town?

How could he have seen it and forgotten it till now? For, technically at least, he should be in possession of all he'd ever known. In that instant back in the hospital it all had come back to him—all that he had been, all that he had done. And if that had been so, why and how had the memory of Willow Grove been withheld from him?

An old town—almost an ancient town—no flying houses perched on their gridded foundation blocks, no airy masses of apartment complexes rising on its outskirts. Solid, honest buildings built of wood and brick and stone, built where they were meant to stay, with no roving tendencies tied into their functions. Some of them, he saw, however, had solar power plants spread awkwardly across their roofs and on the edge of town there had been a larger municipal solar plant, apparently used to pump energy into those houses which were not so equipped.

He shifted the knapsack to a more comfortable position on his shoulder and pulled the cowl of the robe more closely about his face. He crossed the street and wandered slowly up the sidewalk and on every hand were little things that jogged loose memories. There were names now as well as places. Jake Woods had been the banker and Jake Woods could, surely, no longer be alive. For if he had ever seen this town, it must have been more than two centuries ago. And Charley Breen and he had run away from school and gone fishing in the creek and had caught some chubs.

It was incredible, he told himself; it was impossible. And yet the memories kept on piling in on him, not vague and shadowy, but incidents and faces and pictures from the past, all three-dimensional. He remembered that Jake Woods had been lame and had carried a cane and he knew what kind of cane it was—one that was heavy and of a shiny, hand-rubbed wood. Charley had had freckles and a wide, infectious grin, and Charley, he remembered, had always led him into trouble. There had been Minnie Short, an old, befuddled woman, dressed in rags and walking with a weird sort of shuffling trot, who had worked part time as a bookkeeper at the lumber

yard. But the lumber yard was gone and in its place stood
a glass-and-plastic agency for floaters.

He reached a bench that stood in front of a restaurant
across the street from the bank and sat down on it heavily. There were a few people on the street and as they
went past they stared at him.

He felt fine. Even after the hard night of Quester's running, his body still was fresh and strong. Perhaps, he told
himself, it was because of Thinker's stolen energy—an
energy transferred from Thinker to Quester and from
Quester on to him.

He slid the knapsack off his shoulder and let it rest beside him on the bench. He slid the cowl back from his
face.

People were beginning to open up the shops and stores.
A lone car came thrumming gently up the street.

He read the signs and none of them were familiar. The
names of the stores and of the people who owned and op-
erated them all had changed.

On the floor above the bank, the windows bore gilt let-
tering advertising the occupants—dentists, doctors, law-
yers. Alvin Bank, M.D.; H. H. Oliver, Dentistry; Ryan
Wilson, Attorney-at-Law; J. D. Leach, Optometrist; Wm.
Smith——

Wait a minute, there! Back up! Ryan Wilson, that was
it!

Ryan Wilson was the name that had been mentioned in
the message.

There, across the street, was the office of the man who
had indicated in the note that he had something of interest to impart.

The clock above the door of the bank said it was almost nine o'clock. Wilson might be in his office, or would
be coming soon. If the office still were closed, he could
stay and wait for him.

Blake got up off the bench and crossed the street. The

door that opened on the stairs leading to the floor above the bank was rickety and it creaked and groaned as he pushed it open. The stairs were steep and dark and the brown paint that covered the treads was scuffed and peeling off.

Wilson's office was just down the hall, and the door stood open.

Blake went into the outer office, which was empty. In an inner office a man sat in his shirt sleeves, working on some papers, with others stacked high in a basket on the desk.

The man looked up. "Come on in," he said.

"You are Ryan Wilson?"

The man nodded. "My secretary isn't here as yet. What can I do for you?"

"You sent me a message. My name is Andrew Blake."

Wilson leaned back in his chair and stared at him.

"Well, I'll be damned," he finally said. "I never thought I'd see you. I thought you were gone for good."

Blake shook his head, bewildered.

"Have you seen the morning paper?" Wilson asked.

"No," said Blake. "I haven't."

The man reached for a folded copy that lay on the corner of his desk and flicked it open, facing it toward Blake.

The banner screamed:

IS MAN FROM THE STARS A WEREWOLF?

The read-out said:

HUNT STILL GOES ON FOR BLAKE

Plastered underneath the banner, Blake saw, was a picture of himself.

Blake felt his face freezing, fought to keep it frozen, betraying no expression.

Within his brain he felt Quester stirring frantically.

—No! No! He screamed at Quester. Let me handle this.

Quester quieted down.

"It's interesting," Blake said to Wilson. "Thanks for showing me. Have they gotten around to posting a reward?"

Wilson flicked his wrist to fold the paper, put it back on the corner of his desk.

"All you have to do," said Blake, "is dial the phone. The number of the hospital is . . ."

Wilson raised his hand. "It's no concern of mine," he said. "I don't care what you are."

"Even if I were a werewolf."

"Even if you were," said Wilson. "You can turn around and leave if that should be your wish and I'll go back to work. But if you want to stay, there are a couple of questions I am supposed to ask you and if you can answer them . . ."

"Questions?"

"Yes. Just two simple questions."

Blake hesitated.

"I am acting," Wilson told him, "for a client. For a client who died a century and a half ago. This is a matter which has been handed down, generation after generation, within the fabric of this law firm. My great-grandfather was the man who accepted the responsibility of carrying out the request of the client."

Blake shook his head, trying to shake the fog out of his brain. There was something terribly wrong here. He had known it the moment he had seen the town.

"All right," he said. "Go ahead and ask your questions."

Wilson pulled a desk drawer open, took out two envelopes. One he laid aside, the other one he opened, taking out a sheet of paper that crackled when he unfolded it.

The attorney held the sheet in front of him, squinting closely at it.

"All right, Mr. Blake," he said. "First question: What was the name of your first grade teacher?"

"Why, her name was," said Blake, "her name was . . ."

He groped blindly for the answer and all at once he had it.

"Her name was Jones," he said. "Miss Jones. Ada Jones, I think. It was so long ago."

But it was, somehow, not so long ago. Even as he said how long ago it was, he suddenly could see her in his mind. Prim, old-maidish, with a fuzzy hair-do and a stern set to her mouth. And she'd worn a purple blouse. How could he have forgotten that purple blouse she wore?

"O.K.," said Wilson. "What did you and Charley Breen do to Deacon Watson's watermelons?"

"Why," said Blake, "we—say, how did you find out about that one?"

"Never mind," said Wilson. "Just go ahead and answer."

"Well," said Blake, "I guess it was a dirty trick. We both felt badly after we had done it. We never told any one. Charley stole a hypodermic from his father—his old man was a doctor, I suppose you know."

"I don't know a thing," said Wilson.

"Well, we took this syringe and we had a jar of kerosene and we gave each of the melons a squirt of kerosene. We poked the needle through the rind. Not much, you understand. Just enough so the melons would have a funny taste."

Wilson laid down the paper and picked up the other envelope.

"You passed the test," he said. "I guess that this is yours."

He handed the envelope to Blake.

Blake took it and saw that there was writing on its face—the words formed in the shaky penmanship of the very old, the ink faded to a faint, dull brown.

The writing said:

To The Man Who Has My Mind

And underneath that line a signature:

Theodore Roberts

Blake's hand shook and he let it fall straight to his side, still clutching the envelope, and he tried to hold it stiff and straight so it would stop its shaking.

For now he knew—now he knew again, now it was all there, all the things he had forgotten, all the old identities and faces.

"That is me," he said, forcing his stiff lips to move. "That was me. Teddy Roberts. I am not Andrew Blake."

28

He came to the great iron gates, which were locked, went through the postern gate and found the gravel path that went winding up the rise. Below him lay the town of Willow Grove and here, all about him, their places marked by the canted, moss-grown stones, hemmed in by the pines and the ancient fence of iron, lay all those old ones who had been young when he had been a boy.

"Follow the path to the left," Wilson had told him. "You'll find the family plot halfway up the hill, just to the right. But Theodore, you know, is not really dead. He's in the Mind Bank and he's in you as well. It's just his body up there. I don't understand."

"Nor do I," said Blake, "but I feel I have to go."

And so he'd gone, climbing the steep, rough road, seldom used, to the cemetery gates. And as he climbed the hill he thought that of all the town the cemetery looked the most familiar to him. The pine trees, inside the iron fence, were larger and taller than he'd remembered them and, if possible, even in the full light of the day, were darker and more somber than he had thought they'd be. But the wind, moaning through their heavy needles, played a dirge that came straight out of boyhood memories.

Theodore, the letter had been signed. But it had not been Theodore, rather it was Teddy. Little Teddy Roberts, and later on, still Teddy Roberts, young physicist out of Caltech and MIT, before whom the universe had lain a bright and shining mechanism that cried for understanding. The Theodore would come later—Dr. Theodore Roberts, an old and weighty man, with slow step and ponderous voice, and with his hair turned white. And that was a man, Blake told himself, he had never known and would never know. For the mind he carried, the mind that had been impressed upon his synthetic brain, inside his synthetic body, had been the mind of Teddy Roberts.

Now all he needed to do to talk with Teddy Roberts was to pick up a phone and dial the Mind Bank number and identify himself. And then, with a little wait, perhaps, there would be a voice and behind the voice the mind of Theodore Roberts. But not the voice of the man himself, for the voice had been lost in death, nor the mind of Teddy Roberts, but the older, wiser, more steady mind that had grown from the mind of Teddy Roberts. It would do no good, he thought; it would be a stranger talking. Or would it? For it had been Theodore, not Teddy, who had written him the letter, a man writing from his deep old age, the feeble, shaky hand spelling out the greeting and the message.

Could the mind be man? Or was the mind a lonely thing that stood apart from man? How much of man was mind, how much was the body? And how much of humanity did he, himself, represent when he resided as a simple human notion inside of Quester's body—how much less, perhaps, inside of Thinker's body? For Thinker was a being from far outside the human concept, a biological engine that converted energy, with senses that did not entirely correspond with the human sense, with a logic-instinct-wisdom that took the place of mind.

Inside the postern gate he halted and stood in the deep shadow of the pines. The air was heavy with the scent of evergreen and the wind was moaning and far up the hill a man was working among the moss-grown slabs of granite, the sun flashing on the tool he used as he labored in the quietness of the morning light.

The chapel stood beside the gate, the ancient clapboard whiteness of its walls shining in the green shadows of the pines, its steeple stretching upward, trying, but failing, to match the tallness of the trees. Through the open door, Blake glimpsed the soft glow of lights, within.

Walking slowly, Blake went past the chapel and started up the walk. Beneath his feet the gravel grated as it shifted. Halfway up the hill and to the right. And when he got there he'd find the marker that proclaimed quietly to the world that the body of Theodore Roberts lay in the earth beneath.

Blake hesitated.

Why did he want to go?

To visit the place where lay his body—no, not his body, but the body of the man whose mind he wore.

And if that mind were still alive—if two minds were still alive—what did the body matter? It was a husk and its death should occasion no regret and its resting place was of no consequence.

Slowly he turned back down the path, heading for the gate. When he reached the chapel, he stopped and stood looking, through the gate, down upon the town.

He was not ready to go back to the town, he knew—if he ever should be ready. For when he walked into that town again, he must know what to do. And he did not know what to do. He had no ideas what to do.

He turned and went up the walk to the chapel and sat down on the steps.

What should he do now? he wondered. What was left to do?

Now, finally knowing who he was, there was no further need of running. Now he had the ground to stand on, but the ground was meaningless.

He reached into the pocket of his robe and took out the letter. Unfolding it, he sat hunched upon the step, going over it again:

My dear Sir: Which, I suppose, may be a strange and awkward way of addressing you. I have tried other salutations and all of them sounded wrong, so I must fall back upon the one which, while it may seem too formal, at least is dignified.

By now, of course, you know who I am and who you are, so there is no need of any explanation concerning our relationship, which I take to be the first of its kind upon this earth, and perhaps a bit embarrassing to the both of us.

I have lived in hope that someday you would be back and the two of us might sit down, perhaps with drinks in hand, and spend a pleasant hour in comparing notes. Now I have some fear that you may not be coming back, since you have been gone so long, I fear something may have happened that will prevent your coming back. But even if you did, for me to see you your coming must be soon, for the end of life draws near.

The end of life, I say, and yet this is not entirely true. The end of life, of course, so far as I am physically concerned. But my mind will continue to exist in the Intelligence Depository—one mind among many others, able to continue functioning as an independent unit, or acting in collaboration, as a sort of panel or advisory board, with other minds which are existing there.

It has been with some hesitation that I have finally accepted the nomination. I realize, of course, the honor of it, but even having accepted, I am not convinced of the wisdom of it, either for myself or for humanity. I am not certain that a man can live comfortably as a mind alone, and I am afraid, as well, that humanity, in time, may come to depend too heavily upon the accumulated wisdom and knowledge which is contained within the so-called Mind Bank. If we remain, as is the situation today, simply as an advisory board to which questions may be submitted for consideration and recommendation, then the bank may serve a useful purpose. But if the world of men ever comes to depend upon the wisdom of the past alone, glorifying it or deifying it, bowing to it and ignoring the wisdom of their present, then we will become a hindrance and a detriment.

I am not certain why I write you this. Possibly because you are the only one I can write it to—for, in many ways, you are actually myself.

It seems strange that in one lifetime any one man should have been called upon to make two such similar decisions. For when I was selected as the one whose mind should be impressed upon your brain, I felt many of the reservations which I now am feeling. I felt that, in many ways, my mind might not be the kind of mind that would be the best for you. I had prejudices and biases that might be a disservice to pass on. All these years I have not been easy about it, wondering often if my mind had served you well or ill.

Man, indeed, has come far from the simple beast he was when we consider questions such as these. I have sometimes wondered if we might not have come too far, if in the vanity of intelligence we may not be treading upon forbidden ground. But these thoughts have come to me only lately. They are the accumulated doubts of a man who is growing old and so should be discounted.

It must seem to you that this letter is a rambling one, and to little purpose. If you will bear with me, I shall try to get, within a reasonable space of time, to the little purpose it may have.

Through the years I have thought of you often and have wondered how you were, if you were still alive and, if still alive, when you would come back. I think that you must realize by now that some, perhaps even many, of the men who fabricated you thought of you only as a problem in biochemistry. I think that by this time, having lived with it all these years, you will not be disturbed by so frank a statement. I think that you must be the kind of man who would realize it and accept it.

But I have never thought of you in any other way than as another human, in all truth a man very like myself. As you know, I was an only child. I had no brother and no sister. I have often wondered if I have thought of you as the brother that I never had. But in late years I think I know the truth of that. You are not a brother. You are closer than a brother. You are my second self, equal to me in every way and never secondary.

And it is in the hope that, if you do return, even if I physically am dead, you may want to contact me that I write this letter. I am very curious about what you have been doing and what you may be thinking. It has seemed to me that, in view of where you've been and the work you have been doing, you may have developed some interesting and illuminating viewpoints.

Whether you do contact me must be left to your own judgment. I am not entirely sure that the two of us should talk, although I'd like to very much. I'll leave it up to you in all confidence that you'll know what's best to do.

I am, at the moment, very much concerned with the question of whether it is wise for the mind of one man to go on and on. It occurs to me that, while mind may be the greater part of any man, man is not mind alone. There is more involved in man than wisdom and memory and the ability to absorb facts and develop viewpoints. Can a man orient himself in the never-never land such as must exist when the mind alone survives? He may remain a man, of course, but there still is the question of his humanity. Does he become more or less than human?

Perhaps, if you feel it is proper we should talk, you can tell me what you think of all of this.

But if you believe it is better that we remain apart,

please be assured that if I should somehow know, I would understand. And in such a case, I would have you know that my best wishes and my love go with you forever.

Sincerely,
Theodore Roberts

Blake folded the letter and thrust it back into the pocket of his robe.

Still Andrew Blake, he thought, and not Theodore Roberts. Teddy Roberts, maybe, but never Theodore Roberts.

And if he sat down before a phone and dialed the Mind Bank number, what would he have to say when Theodore Roberts came upon the line? What could he say? For he had nothing he could offer. They would be two men, each needing help, each looking to the other for the help that neither one could give.

He could say: I am a werewolf—that's what the papers call me. I am only part a man, no more than one third a man. The rest of me is something else, something that you've never heard of, something that you could not credit, having heard of it. I am no longer human and there's no place here for me, no place upon the earth. I belong nowhere. I'm a monster and a freak and I can only hurt anyone I touch.

And that was right. He would hurt anyone he touched. Elaine Horton, who had kissed him—a girl that he could love, that he perhaps already loved. Although he could love her only with the human part of him, with one third of him. And he could hurt her father, that marvellous old man with the ramrod back and the ramrod principles. And hurt as well that young doctor, Daniels, who had been his first, and for a time, his only friend.

He could hurt them all—he would hurt them all unless . . .

And that was it. Unless.

There was something he must do, some action he must take.

He searched his mind for this thing that he must do and it was not there.

He rose slowly from the steps and turned toward the gate, then turned back again and went into the chapel, pacing slowly down the aisle.

The place was hushed and shadowed. An electric candelabra, mounted on the lectern, did little to drive back the shadows, a feeble campfire glow burning in the darkened emptiness of a desolated plain.

A place to think. A place to scheme, to huddle for a time. A place to array his thoughts and align the situation and see what he must do.

He reached the front of the building and moved over from the aisle to sit down on one of the seats. But he did not sit down. He remained standing, buttressed by the twilit quiet—a quiet that was emphasized rather than broken by the soft sound of the wind in the pines outside.

This was the decision point, he knew. Here, finally, he had come to that time and place from which there was no retreat. He had run before, and ran to a certain purpose, but now there was no longer any virtue in the simple and impulsive act of fleeing. For there was no longer any place to flee to—he had reached the ultimate point and now, if he were to run again, he must know what he was running to.

Here, in this little town, he had found who and what he was and this town was a dead-end. The whole planet was a dead-end and there was no place for him upon this earth, no place for him in humanity.

For while he was of earth, he could lay no claim to humanity. He was a hybrid, rather—out of man's terrible scheming had arisen something that had not heretofore existed.

He was a team, a team of three different beings. That team had the opportunity and the capacity to work upon, and perhaps to solve, a basic universal problem, but it was not a problem that had specifically to do with the planet Earth or the life that resided on the Earth. He could do nothing here and nothing could be done for him.

On some other planet, perhaps, a bleak and barren planet where there'd be interference, where there was no culture and no cultural distraction—perhaps there he could perform the function—he, the team, not he the human, but he, the three of them together.

Out of the mists of time and distance he remembered once again the headiness of the realization, when it had come to them, that within their grasp lay the possibility of resolving the purpose and the meaning of the universe. Or if not of solving it, of digging closer to the core of it than any intelligence had ever dug before.

He thought again of what lay in the power of those three minds that had been linked together by the unconscious and unintending ingenuity shaped by the minds of men—the power and the beauty, the wonder and the awfulness. And he quailed before the realization that, perhaps, here had been forged an instrument that outraged all the purpose and the meaning for which it now could seek throughout the universe.

In time, perhaps, the three minds would become a single mind and if that should happen, then his humanity would no longer matter, for it would be gone. Then the ties that bound him to a planet called the Earth and to the race of bipedal beings that resided upon the earth would be snapped and he would be free. Then, he told himself, he could rest easy, then he could forget. And then, perhaps, when he had forgotten, when he was no longer human, he could look upon the powers and capabilities held within that common mind as nothing more than commonplace. For the mind of man, he knew, while it might be clever, was very limited. It gaped at wonder and boggled at the full concept of the universe. But while it might be limited, he told himself, it was safe and warm and comfortable.

He had outgrown the humanity with which he had been endowed and that outgrowing hurt. It left him weak and empty, outside the comfort and the warmth.

He crouched upon the floor and wrapped his arms about him. This little space, he thought, even this tiny room which, crouched, he occupied—even this space did not belong to him nor did he belong to it. There was nowhere for him. He was a tangled nothingness which had been spawned by accident. He had never been meant to be. He was an intruder. An intruder, perhaps, upon this planet only, but the humanity that still clung to him made this planet matter—the only place in all the universe that mattered.

In time he might shuck off the humanness, but that, if ever, would be millenia from now. And it mattered to him now. Now and the Earth, not forever and the universe.

He felt the sympathy reaching out for him and he knew dimly where it came from and even in his bitterness and despair, he knew it was a trap and cried out against it.

He struggled feebly, but they still kept reaching out to snare him and he heard the words and thoughts that passed between the two of them and the words that they spoke to him, although he did not understand them.

They reached out and took him and folded him close against them and their alien warmth held him secure and tight and safe.

He sank into the comfort of forgetting and the battered core of his agony seemed to melt away in a world where there was nothing but the three of them—just he and those two others, bound together for all eternity.

29

A December wind, sharp-toothed and thin, keened across the land, stripping the last of the brown and shriveled leaves from the lone oak tree that stood halfway up the hill. Atop the hill, where the cemetery stood, the giant pines moaned in the chill of the dying year. Ragged clouds raced across the sky and there was a smell of coming snow riding on the wind. Two trim blue figures stood at the cemetery gates, the pale winter sunlight, shining for a moment through the broken clouds, gleaming off the polished buttons and the rifle barrels. To one side of the gate a small group of sight-seers huddled, peering through the iron bars at the whiteness of the chapel.

"Not many here today," Ryan Wilson told Elaine Horton. "When the weather was good, especially on weekends, we had quite a crowd."

He shucked the collar of his grey robe close about his neck.

"Not that I approve of it," he said. "That's Theodore Roberts up there. I don't care what shape he takes, it still is Theodore Roberts."

"Dr. Roberts, I take it," said Elaine, "was well thought of in Willow Grove."

"That he was," said Wilson. "He was the only one of us who ever gained distinction. The town is proud of him."

"And you resent all this?"

"I don't know if you can say resentment. So long as a proper decorum is maintained, I don't think we mind.

But at times the crowds take on a holiday aspect and that we do not like."

"Perhaps," said Elaine, "I should not have come. I thought a long time about it. But the more I thought about it, the more it seemed I must."

"You were his friend," said Wilson gravely. "You have a right to come. I don't imagine he had too many friends."

The small crowd of huddled people had drifted from the gates and was starting down the hill.

"On a day like this," said Wilson, "there's not much for them to see. So they don't stay very long. Just the chapel. In the good weather, of course, the chapel doors were open and you could catch a glimpse inside. But even then, there wasn't much to see. To begin with just a patch of darkness, a patch of nothingness, and you couldn't always see it. But now, when the doors are open, you get a sense of shining, of something shining there. At first it didn't shine. You couldn't see a thing. Just like looking into a hole that hung just above the floor. Everything blotted out. A shield of some sort, I suppose. But now, gradually, the shield, the defenses, whatever they may be, have been dropped and you can see it shining there."

"Will they let me in?" Elaine asked.

"I think they will," said Wilson. "I'll send word to the captain. You can't blame Space Administration for clamping down so hard. The responsibility for whatever's up there rests solely with them. They started the project, two hundred years ago. What happened here would not have happened if it hadn't been for Project Werewolf."

Elaine shuddered.

"You'll pardon me," said Wilson. "I should not have said that."

"Why shouldn't you?" she asked. "Unpleasant as it is, that's what it's called by everyone."

"I told you about that day he came into the office," Wilson said. "He was a nice young man."

"He was a frightened man," said Elaine, "running from the world. If he had only told me . . ."

"Perhaps then he didn't know . . ."

"He knew he was in trouble. The senator and I would have helped him. Dr. Daniels would have helped him."

"He didn't want to involve you. It was not the sort of thing one would involve his friends in. And he wanted to keep your friendship. He was afraid, more than likely, if he told you, that he would lose the friendship."

"I can see," said Elaine, "how he might have thought so. And I didn't even try to make him tell me. I blame myself for that. But I didn't want to hurt him. I thought he should have a chance of finding the answer for him-self."

The crowd came down the hill, went by the two of them and continued down the road.

30

The pyramid stood to the left, and in front of the row of seats. It glowed dully, pulsating slightly, and out from it hung a curtain of light.

"Don't go too close," the captain said. "You might frighten it."

Elaine did not answer. She stared at the pyramid and the horror and the wonder of it rose in her throat to choke her.

"You can go down two or three more rows of seats," the captain said. "It might be dangerous if you tried to get too close. We don't really know."

Words forced themselves up and out of her. "Frighten it?" she asked.

"I don't know," the captain said. "That's the way it acts. As if it might be frightened of us. Or suspicious of us. Or maybe just doesn't want anything to do with us. It wasn't like this until recently. It was blacked out, a piece of emptiness, as if there were nothing there. Creating a world of its own, with all defenses up."

"And now he knows that we won't harm him?"

"Him?"

"Andrew Blake," she said.

"You knew him, miss? Mr. Wilson said so."

"I saw him three times," she said.

"About knowing we won't hurt him," the captain said. "Maybe that is it. Some of the scientists think so. A lot of them have tried to study it—pardon me, Miss

Horton—have tried to study him. But they don't get too far. Nothing much to work on."

"They're sure?" she asked. "They're sure it's Andrew Blake?"

"Down underneath the pyramid," the captain told her. "Down at the base of it, on the right hand side."

"The robe!" she cried. "That was the one I gave him!"

"Yes. The one that he was wearing. It's down there on the floor. Just the corner of it sticking out."

She took a step down the aisle.

"Not too far," the captain warned. "Not too close."

She took another step and halted.

This is foolish, she thought. If he is there, he knows. He'd know that it is me and he would not be frightened—he'd know I have for him nothing but my love.

The pyramid pulsated gently.

But perhaps he doesn't know, she told herself. Perhaps he has locked himself against the world and if that is what he's done, he had reason to.

How must it be, she wondered, to know that your mind is the mind of another man—a loaned mind since you can have none of your own, because man's ingenuity was not quite great enough to fabricate a mind? Ingenuity sufficient to fashion bone and flesh and brain, but not to fashion mind. And how much worse, perhaps, to know that you were a part of two other minds—at least two other minds.

"Captain?" she asked.

"Yes, Miss Horton."

"Do the scientists know how many minds there are? Could it be more than three?"

"They don't seem to know," he said. "Granted the situation as it stands, there might not be a limit."

No limit, she thought. Room for an infinity of minds, for all the thought that lay in the universe.

I am here, she said, speaking silently to the creature that had been Andrew Blake. I am here. Can't you tell I'm here? If you ever need me, if you change back into a man again . . .

But why should he change back into a man again? Perhaps he had changed to this so he need not be a man, so that he need not face a humanity that he could not share.

She turned and took a hesitant step toward the chapel's front, then turned back once more.

The pyramid was shining softly and it seemed so peaceful and so solid, yet withdrawn, that her throat constricted and tears came to her eyes.

I will not weep, she told herself, fiercely. I will not weep, for whom would I be weeping? For Andrew Blake? For myself? For the befuddled race of man?

Not dead, she thought. But worse than death, perhaps. If he had been a man and dead, she could have walked away. She could have said goodbye.

Once he had turned to her for help. Now he was beyond her help, or any human help. Perhaps, she thought, he was beyond all humanity.

She turned again.

"I'll leave now," she said. "Captain, please, would you walk beside me."

He took her arm and walked beside her up the aisle.

31

It all was there. The great black towers anchored in the planet's granite crust, reached toward the skies. The green and leafy glade, with its flowers and gaily-playing animals, stood motionless in time. The pink-white structure rose in airy curves and spirals above the purple, foam-flecked sea. And in the aridity of the great plateau the mustard-colored domes of hermit intelligences ran as far as sense could reach.

These and many others—and not the pictures of them only, snatched from the ice-hard stars which lay like scattered crystals across the skies that roofed a planet of drifted sand and snow—but the ideas and the thoughts and concepts that clung to all the pictures, like bits of dirt to roots.

Most of the thoughts and concepts were simply isolated pieces which would not correlate, but all of them were springboards for the fabrication of a vast jigsaw puzzle net of logic.

The task was an enormous one and at times confusing, but bit by bit the various data fell into filing patterns, and once identified were erased from active consideration, but still tagged and available when there should be need of them.

It worked with satisfaction and a happiness—and that bothered it. Satisfaction was all right and quite permissible, but happiness was wrong. It was something that had been unknown and should not be felt; it was an alien thing and it was emotion. For the best result, there must be nothing like emotion, and it was irritated at the happiness and tried to wipe it out.

A contagion, it told itself. A contagion that it had caught from Changer and, as well, perhaps, from Quester, who was at the best a most unstable creature. A situation that it must guard against, for happiness was bad enough—there were other illogical emotions held by those two that could be even worse.

So it wiped away the happiness and posted guard against it, and went on with its work, reducing the ideas and the thoughts and concepts, insofar as they could be so reduced, to formulae and axioms and symbols, being careful in the process not to lose the substance of them, for the substance would be needed later.

There were tantalizing hints that must be docketed for more consideration and, perhaps, even for more data. The logic pattern potentially was sound, but extrapolated too far it left some room for error and needed further data to indicate direction. There were so many tricky things; there was nothing ever easy. The process called for hard discipline and constant self-examination to be certain that the concept of one's self was eliminated. That was the thing, it thought, that made the happiness so bad.

The material of that black tower, for example. So thin it seemed impossible for it to stand, let alone have strength. But there could be no doubt about its thinness; that information came through very clear and solid. But the hint of neutrons was something else—neutrons packed so solidly together that they assumed the characteristics of a metal, all held in a rigid association by a force for which there was no definition. The hint indicated time, but was time a force? A dislocated time, perhaps. A time straining to take its proper place in either past or future, forever striving toward a goal made impossible by some fantastic mechanism that kept time out of step?

And the fishers of space who cast their nets across empty cubic light-years, catching the energy spewed out in space by all the angry suns. Catching, in the process, the incredible flotsam of unknown things that once had crossed or once had lived in space—the garbage of the vast stretches of abandoned space. Nothing about the fishers or what kind of nets they cast or how these nets might trap the energy. Just the thought that the fishers fished. Some fantasy, perhaps of some dim communal mind, a religion or a faith or myth—or could there be the fishers?

These and many more and that one faint impression, so faint it barely registered, faint, perhaps, because it had been dredged from a star so distant that even light grew tired. A universal mind, it said, and that was all it said. A mind, perhaps, from which all thinking came. A mind, perhaps, that gathered in all thinking. Or a mind that set the law and order which spun the electron around the nucleus and called out marching cadences to the galaxies.

There was much, and all of it fragmentary and very puzzling. And this was just a start. This was the harvest merely of a moment of time on a single planet. But it was important, all of it, every bit of information, every faint impression. Somewhere it all fit in, somehow there was a place for it in that pattern of law and order, cause and effect, action and reaction which made up the universe.

Time was all that was needed. With more data and more logic it could all become as one. And time, as a factor, could be canceled out. There was an eternity of it.

Thinker, squatted on the chapel floor, pulsated gently, the logic mechanism that was its mind driving toward the universal truth.

32

Changer struggled.

He must get out. He must escape. He could not remain, buried in this blackness and quietness, in the comfort and security, in the brotherhood that encompassed and engulfed him.

He did not want to struggle. He would rather have stayed exactly where he was, remain the thing he was. But something made him struggle—not something inside himself, it seemed, but something from outside himself, a creature or a being or a situation that called out to him and told him that he could not stay, that no matter how much he might wish to stay, he could not. There was something left undone and it could not be left undone and he was the only one who would be able to perform the task, whatever it might be.

—Quiet, quiet, said Quester. You are better where you are. There is too much grief, too much bitterness for you outside of here.

Outside of here? he wondered. And remembered some of it. A woman's face, the tall pines at the gate—another world seen as one would see it through a wall of running water, remote and far away and improbable. But he knew that it was there.

—You shut me in! he shouted. You must let me go.

But Thinker paid no attention to him. Thinker went on thinking, all his energies directed toward the many pieces of information and of fact—the great black towers, the mustard-colored domes, the hint of something or some-one barking out the orders for the universe.

His strength and will wore off and he sank into the blackness and the quiet.

—Quester, he said.

—No, said Quester. Thinker's hard at work.

He lay and raged wordlessly at the two of them, raging in his mind. But raging did no good.

I did not treat them that way, he told himself. When I was in the body, I listened to them always. I did not shut them out.

He lay and rested and the thought was in his mind that it was better to stay in the comfort and the quietness. What did this other matter, whatever it might be? What did Earth matter?

And there he had it—Earth!

Earth and humanity. And the both of them did matter. Not, perhaps, to Quester or to Thinker—although what mattered to the one of them must matter to all three.

He struggled feebly and he did not have the strength, nor perhaps the will.

So he lay back again and waited, gathering strength and patience.

They cared for him, he told himself. They had reached out and taken him in an hour of anguish and now they held him close, for healing, and they would not let him go.

He tried to call up the anguish once again in the hope that in the anguish he would find the strength and will. But he could not recall it. It had been wiped away. He could claw at the edges of it, but could not get a grip upon it.

So he snuggled close against the darkness and let the quiet come in, but even as he did he knew that he would struggle to break free again, feebly, perhaps, hoping, more than likely, that he would not succeed, but knowing that he must keep on and on, never ceasing, because there was some not entirely understood, but compelling reason that he should.

He lay quietly and thought how like a dream it was, a dream wherein one climbed a mountain, but could never reach the top, or one in which one clung to a precipice until his fingers slipped and then fell endlessly, filled with the terror of the falling and of hitting bottom, but never reaching bottom.

Time and futility stretched out ahead of him and time itself, he knew, was futile, for he knew what Thinker knew—that time was not a factor.

He tried to put his situation into correct perspective, but it refused to fall into a pattern against which perspective could be measured. Time was a blur and reality a haze and swimming down toward him through the haze came a face—a face that at first meant not too much to him, but, finally, he realized, of someone that he knew, and then, at last, a face, half seen in darkness, that was imprinted on his mind forever.

The lips moved and he could not hear the words, but they, too, the memory of them, was blazoned in his mind.

When you can, they said, *let me hear from you.*

And that was it, he thought. He had to let her know. She was waiting to hear what had happened to him.

He surged up out of the darkness and the quiet and there seemed to be a roaring all about him—the outraged roaring protest of the other two.

Black towers spun in the darkness all about him— black spinning in the dark, with the sense of motion, but no sight. And suddenly sight as well.

He stood in the chapel and the place was dim with the feeble light of the candelabra and from outside he could hear the moaning of the pines.

There was someone shouting and he saw a soldier running up the aisle toward the front, while another stood, startled, with his rifle raised.

"Captain! Captain!" bawled the running man.

The other soldier took a short step forward.

"Take it easy, son," said Blake. "I'm not going anywhere."

There was something tangled about his ankles and he saw it was his robe. He kicked it free and reached down to lift it and hang it on his shoulders.

A man with bars upon his shoulders came striding down the aisle. He stopped in front of Blake.

"I am Captain Saunders, sir," he said. "Space Administration. We have been guarding you."

"Guarding me?" asked Blake. "Or watching me?"

The captain grinned, just slightly. "Perhaps a bit of both," he said. "May I congratulate you, sir, on becoming human once again."

Blake pulled the robe more tightly about his shoulders. "You are wrong," he said. "You must know by now you're wrong. You know I am not human—not entirely human."

Perhaps, he thought, only human in the shape he now possessed. Although there must be more to it than that, for he'd been designed as human, had been engineered as human. There had been change, of course, but not so much change that he was un-human. Just un-human enough, he thought, to be unacceptable. Just un-human enough to be viewed as a monster by humanity.

"We've been waiting," said the captain. "We've been hoping . . ."

"How long?" asked Blake. "How long has it been?"

"Almost a year," the captain said.

A year! thought Blake. It had not seemed that long. It had seemed no more than hours. How long, he wondered, had he been held, unknowing, in the healing depths of the communal mind before he had come to know that he must break free? Or had he known from the first and struggled from the moment that Thinker had superceded him? It was hard to know, he realized. Time, inside the disassociated mind, might be robbed entirely of its meaning, might become useless as a yardstick for duration.

But long enough, at least, to effect some healing, for now the terror and the sharp-edged agony was gone, now he could stand and face the prospect that he was not human in sufficient measure to claim a place upon the Earth.

"And now?" he asked.

"My orders," the captain said, "are to take you to Washington, to Space Administration, as soon as it is safe to do so."

"It is safe right now," Blake told him. "I will cause no trouble."

"It's not you I mean," the captain said. "It's the crowd outside."

"What do you mean—a crowd?"

"This time a crowd of worshipers. There are cults, it seems, which think you are a messiah sent to deliver Man from all the evil in him. And at other times there are other groups that denounce you as a monster— You'll pardon me, please, sir. I forgot myself."

"These groups," said Blake, "the both of them, have given you some trouble?"

"At times," the captain said. "At times a great deal of it. That is why we must sneak out of here."

"But wouldn't it be better to just walk out? Put an end to it?"

"Unfortunately," said the captain, "it's not a situation that can be handled quite so easily. I may as well be frank with you. No one except a few of us will know that you are gone. The guard will still be kept and . . ."

"You'll go on letting the people think that I'm still here?"

"Yes. It will be simpler that way."

"But someday . . ."

The captain shook his head. "No. Not for a long, long time. You will not be seen. We have a ship waiting for you. So that you can leave—if you want to go, of course."

"To get rid of me?"

"Perhaps," the captain said. "But it also will enable you to get rid of us."

33

Earth wanted to get rid of him, perhaps afraid of him, perhaps merely disgusted by him, a loathsome product of its own ambitions and imagination that must be quickly swept underneath the rug. For there was no place for him on the Earth or in humanity, and yet he was a human product and had been made possible by the nimble brains and the weasel understanding of Earth's scientists.

He had wondered at this and thought of it when he first had gone into the chapel and now, standing at the window of his room and looking out at the streets of Washington, he knew he had been right, that he had judged accurately the reaction of humanity.

Although how much of this attitude was the actual attitude of the people of the world, how much the official attitude of Space Administration, there was no way of knowing. To Space he was an old mistake, a planning gone far wrong, and the quicker he could be gotten rid of, the better it would be.

There had been, he remembered, a crowd on the hillside outside the cemetery—a crowd that had gathered there to pay homage to what they thought he stood for. Crackpots, certainly, cultists, more than likely—the kind of people who leaped at any new sensation to fill their empty lives, but still people, still human beings, still humanity.

He stood and stared out at the sun-drenched streets of Washington, with the few cars moving up and down the avenue, and the lazy strollers who sauntered on the sidewalks underneath the trees. The Earth, he thought, the Earth and the people living on it—people who had their jobs and a family to go home to, who had chores and hobbies, their worries and their little triumphs, and their friends. But people who belonged. Even if he could belong, he wondered, if by some circumstance beyond imagining, he should be made acceptable to humanity, could he consider it? For he was not himself alone. He could not consider himself alone, for there were the other two and they held with him, in joint right, this mass of matter which made up his body.

That he was caught up in an emotional trap was no concern of theirs, although back there in the chapel they had made it concern of theirs. That they, themselves, were incapable of such emotion was beside the point— although, thinking of it, he wondered if Quester might not hold as great an emotional capacity as he.

But to become an outcast, to be ejected out of Earth, to roam the universe a pariah out of Earth, seemed more than he could face.

The ship was waiting for him, almost ready now, and it was up to him—he could go or stay. Although Space had made it quite apparent it was preferred that he should go.

And there was, actually, nothing to be gained by staying, only the faint hope that some day he might become a human once again.

And if he could—if he only could—would he want it?

His brain hummed with the absence of an answer and he stood, looking dully out the window, only half-seeing what lay out on the street.

A knock on the door brought him around.

The door came open and through it he saw the guard, standing in the hallway.

Then a man was coming in and for a moment, half-blinded from looking out the window at the bright glare of the street, Blake did not recognize him. Then he saw who it was.

"Senator," he said, moving toward the man, "it was kind of you to come. I hadn't thought you would."

"Why shouldn't I have come?" asked Horton. "Your message said you'd like to talk with me."

"I didn't know if you would want to see me," Blake told him. "After all, I probably contributed to the outcome of the referendum."

"Perhaps," Horton agreed. "Yes, perhaps you did. Stone was most unethical in his use of you as a horrible example. Although I must give the man his due—he used it most effectively."

"I'm sorry," said Blake. "That's what I want to tell you. I would have come to see you, but it seems that, for the moment, I am under a mild sort of detention."

"Well, now," said Horton, "I would think there'd be more to talk about than that. The referendum and its consequences are, as you may guess, a rather painful subject for me. I sent in my resignation just the other day. It will take a little time, quite frankly, to get used to not being a senator."

"Won't you have a seat?" asked Blake. "The chair over there, perhaps. And I can find some brandy."

"That is an idea," said the senator, "that I can heartily subscribe to. It's late enough in the afternoon to begin one's drinking for the day. That time you came to the house, you may recall, we had brandy then. If I remember, it was a rather special bottle."

He sat down in the chair and looked around the room.

"I must say," he declared, "they're doing well for you. Officer's quarters, no less."

"And a guard at the door," said Blake.

"They're a bit afraid of you, more than likely."

"I suppose they may be. But there's no need of it."

Blake went to the liquor cabinet and got out a bottle

and two glasses. He came back across the room and sat down on a sofa, facing Horton.

"I understand," said the senator, "that you're on the point of leaving us. The ship, I'm told, is almost ready."

Blake nodded, pouring out the brandy. He handed the senator a glass.

"I've been doing some wondering about the ship," he said. "No crew. Just me alone in it. Entirely automatic. To accomplish all of this in just one year's time . . ."

"Oh, not a year's time," the senator protested. "Hasn't anyone taken the time to tell you about the ship?"

Blake shook his head. "They've briefed me. That's the word—briefed. I've been told what levers to push and what dials to spin to take me where I want to go. How the food processors work. The housekeeping of the ship. But that is all they've told me. I asked, of course, but there seemed to be no answers. The main point seemed to be to give me the bum's rush off the Earth."

"I see," said the senator. "The old military game. A holdover from the old days. Channels and things like that, I would imagine. And a bit, as well, more than likely, of their ridiculous security."

He swirled the brandy in his glass, looked up at Blake. "You needn't be afraid of it, if that's what's in your mind. It isn't any trap. It'll do all the things they say it will."

"I'm glad to hear that, senator."

"That ship wasn't built," said the senator. "You might say that it was grown. It's been continuously on the drawing boards for forty years or more. Redesigned again and yet again. Built and then torn down to incorporate improvements or a new design. Tested time and time again. An attempt, you see, to build a perfect ship. Millions of man-days and billions of dollars spent on it. And always, you see, at any time, within a year or so of being finished because the refinements they were building into it finally became just that—refinements. It is a ship that can operate forever and a man can live in it forever. It is the one way a person equipped as you are can go out in space and do the job he's built to do."

Blake crinkled his brow. "One thing, senator. Why go to all the bother?"

"Bother? I don't understand."

"Well, look—what you say is right. That strange creature of which we're talking—of which I am a third—can go out in such a ship to roam the universe, to do our job. But what's the pay-off? What's in it for the human race? Do you believe, perhaps, that some day we'll come sailing back across mega-light-years to hand over to you all that we have learned?"

"I don't know," said the senator. "Maybe that's the thought. Maybe you might even do it. Maybe there's enough humanity in you that you will come back."

"I doubt it, senator."

"Well," said the senator, "there's not much point in talking of it. Perhaps, even were you willing, it would be impossible. We are aware of the time your work will involve and mankind's not so stupid—or I don't think we are so stupid—as to imagine that we will last forever. By the time you have your answer, if you ever get an answer, there may be no human race."

"We'll get the answer. If we go out, we'll get the answer."

"Another thing," said the senator. "Has it occurred to you that humanity might be capable of sending you out, of making it possible for you to go out in space to hunt for your answer, even if we knew we would not benefit? Knowing that somewhere in the universe there'd be some intelligence to which your data and your answer would be useful."

"I hadn't thought of that," said Blake, "and I'm not sure that I believe it."

"You're bitter toward us, aren't you."

"I'm not sure," said Blake. "I don't know what I feel. A man who has come home again and is not allowed to stay. Who is kicked out almost the moment he arrives."

"You don't have to go, of course. I had thought you wanted to. But if you want to stay . . ."

"Stay for what?" cried Blake. "To be cooped up in a pretty cage in full official kindness? To be stared and pointed at? To have fools kneel outside your cage as they knelt and prayed on that hillside back in Willow Grove?"

"It would be rather pointless, I suppose," said Horton. "Staying here, I mean. Out in space you'd have at least a job to do and . . ."

"That's another thing," said Blake. "How come you know so much about me? How did you dig it out? How did you figure out what was actually involved?"

"I understand," said Horton, "that it was a matter of basic deduction, based on intensive observation and research. But we'd not got anywhere without the Brownies' help."

So that was it, thought Blake. The Brownies once again.

"They were interested in you," said Horton. "They're interested, it seems, in everything alive. Meadow mice, insects, porcupines—even human beings. I suppose you could call them psychologists. Although that's not the proper word. Their ability goes far beyond psychology."

"It wasn't me, of course," said Blake. "Not Andrew Blake, I mean."

"No. As Andrew Blake, you were just another human. But they sensed the three of you—long before we knew about the three of you, although we eventually would have known. They spent a lot of time with Thinker. Just squatting there and looking at him, although I suspect they were doing more than looking."

"So between the two of you, the humans and the Brownies, you got the basic facts."

"Not all of them," said Horton, "but enough to know the abilities you possessed and what you could do with them. We realized those capabilities must not be wasted. You had to have a chance to use them. And we suspected, too, that you could not use them here on Earth. That's when Space decided to let you have the ship."

"So it boils down to this," said Blake. "I have a job to do. Whether I want to or not, there's a job to do."

Horton said, a little stiffly: "I suppose it's up to you."

"It was not a job I asked for."

"No," Horton agreed. "No, I guess you didn't. But there must be some satisfaction in its magnitude."

They sat for a moment, silent, both of them uneasy at how the talk had turned. Horton finished the brandy and set the glass aside. Blake reached for the bottle.

Horton shook his head. "No, thank you. I must be going soon. But before I go, there is a question. It's this: What do you expect to find out there? What do you know already?"

"As to what we expect," said Blake, "I have no idea. As to what we know—a lot of things that add up to nothing."

"No hint? No idea of what it might all add up to? No pattern starting to emerge?"

"There's one indication. Not too strong, but there. A universal mind."

"You mean a mind that operates the universe—that pushes all the necessary buttons?"

"Maybe," said Blake. "Maybe something like that."

Horton let out his breath. "Oh, my God!" he said.

"Yes—oh, my God," said Blake, not mocking, but very close to mockery.

Horton rose stiffly. "I must go," he said. "Thank you for the drink."

"Senator," said Blake, "I sent a message to Elaine and there was no answer. I tried to telephone."

"Yes," said Horton, "I am aware of that."

"I must see her, sir. Before I go. There are certain things I want to say to . . ."

"Mr. Blake," said Horton, "my daughter does not wish to see you, nor to speak with you."

Blake rose slowly to face him. "But what is the reason? Can you tell me why?"

"I should think," said Horton, "even to you, the reason must be obvious."

34

The shadows crept into the room and Blake still sat upon the couch, unstirring, his brain still beating its weary circle about the one uncompromising fact.

She did not want to see or talk with him—and it had been the memory of her face that had finally brought him surging up out of the darkness and the quiet. If what the senator had said was true, then all the longing and the effort had been for nothing. He might better have stayed where he was until Thinker had finished with his cogitation and his calculation, lying there and healing.

But had the senator spoken the truth? Did he harbor some resentment for the part that Blake had played in the defeat of the bioengineering project? Had he taken this way to pay back, at least in part, the disappointment he had suffered?

This did not seem too likely, Blake told himself, for the senator surely knew enough of politics to have realized that the bioengineering business had been a gamble at the best. And there was something strange about it all. To start with, Horton had been affable and had brushed off mention of the referendum, then suddenly had turned brusque and cold. Almost as if he had been playing a part well thought-out beforehand, although such a thing as that simply made no sense.

—You are taking it most excellently, said Thinker. No pulling of the hair, no gnashing of the teeth, no moaning.

—Oh, shut up! snapped Quester. Leave the man alone.

—I but sought to pay a compliment, persisted Thinker,

and to offer moral support. He approaches it on a high, cerebral level, without emotional outburst. That is the only way to bring solution to a problem such as this.

Thinker gave a mental sigh.

—Although, he said, I must admit I cannot untangle the importance of this problem.

—Don't pay attention to him, Quester said to Blake. Any decision that you come to will be O.K. with me. If you wish to remain on this planet for a time, I would not mind at all. We could manage it.

—Oh, surely, Thinker said. There would be no problem. What is one human lifetime? You would not want to stay more than one human lifetime, would you?

"Sir," asked the Room, "shall I turn on the lights?"

"No," said Blake. "Not yet."

"But it is becoming dark, sir."

"I do not mind the dark," said Blake.

"Would you care for supper, then?"

"Not at the moment, thank you."

"Kitchen could make whatever you might like."

"In a while," said Blake. "I am not hungry yet."

They had said that they would not mind if he should want to stay on Earth, if he should decide to have a try at becoming human, but what would be the use?

—You could try, said Quester. The female human might decide to change her mind.

—I don't think she will, said Blake.

And that, of course, was the worst of it, that he could understand why she wouldn't change her mind, why she should want nothing to do with a being such as he.

But it was not Elaine only, although she was, he knew, the greater part of it. It was, as well, the matter of cutting the final tie with these people to whom he could claim a kinship, the hankering for the home that he had never had, but that the humanity which was in him cried out should be his, of being forced to give up a birthright before he had a chance to claim it. And that was it, he told himself—the home, the birthright and the kinfolk were the more precious to him because, deep within his heart, he knew that he could never have them.

A bell tinkled softly.

The Room said, "The phone is ringing, sir."

He slid along the sofa until he was in front of it. His hand reached out and flipped the toggle. The screen flickered and kept on flickering, but there was no image.

"This call," said the voice of the operator, "must be made without visual transmission. It is within your right to refuse acceptance of it."

"No," said Blake. "Go ahead. It makes no difference to me."

A voice, concise and frosty, speaking flat words, with no hint of intonation, said: "This is the mind of Theodore Roberts speaking. You are Andrew Blake?"

"Yes," said Blake. "How are you, Dr. Roberts?"

"I am all right. How could I be otherwise?"

"I am sorry. I forgot. I did not think."

"You had not contacted me, so I am contacting you. I think that we should talk. I understand you will be leaving soon."

"The ship," said Blake, "is almost ready for me."

"You go to learn."

"That is right," said Blake.

"The three of you?"

"The three of us," said Blake.

"I have thought of that often," said the mind of Theodore Roberts, "ever since I was informed of your situation. The day will come, of course, when there'll not be three of you, but one."

"I had thought that, too," said Blake. "It will take a long, long time."

"Time has no meaning to you," said the mind of Theodore Roberts. "To either one of us. You have an immortal body that can only die by violence. I have no body and thus am immune to violence. The only thing that can kill me is the failure of the technology that supports my mind.

"And Earth has no meaning, either. I think it is important for you to recognize this fact. Earth is no more than a point in space—a tiny point in space, and insignificant.

"There is so little in this universe, once you think of it, that really matters. When you sift down to the bottom of it, all that really counts is intelligence. If you are looking for a common denominator in the universe, seek intelligence."

"The human race?" asked Blake. "Humanity? It does not matter, either?"

"The human race," said the precise, frosty voice, "is a splinter of intelligence, not as a human being, not as any kind of being."

"But intelligence . . ." Blake began, then stopped.

It was useless, he told himself, to try to present another viewpoint to this thing with which he spoke, not a man, but a disembodied mind which was as biased in its environment as a being of flesh and blood would be biased by its environment. Lost to the physical world, remembering the physical world as dimly, perhaps, as a grown man might recall his babyhood, the mind of Theodore Roberts existed in a world of only one dimension. A small world with flexible parameters, but a world in which nothing happened except it happened as an intellectual exercise.

"What was that you said—or meant to say?"

"I suppose," said Blake, ignoring the question, "that you tell me this . . ."

"I tell you this," said Theodore Roberts, "because I know you must be sorely tried and very greatly puzzled. And since you are part of me . . ."

"I am not a part of you," said Blake. "You gave me a

mind, two centuries ago. That mind has changed. It's not your mind any more."

"I had thought . . ." said Theodore Roberts.

"I know. It was kind of you. But it isn't any good. I stand on my two feet. I have to. There is no choice. Too many people had a hand in me and I can't tear myself apart to give each one of them their due—not you, not the biologists who drew the blueprints, not the technicians who formed the bone and flesh and nerve."

There was a silence then and Blake said, quickly: "I'm sorry. Perhaps I should not have said that. I hope you are not angry."

"Not angry," said the mind of Theodore Roberts. "Gratified, perhaps. Now I need no longer worry, wondering if my biases and my prejudices might be of disservice to you. But I have allowed myself to ramble on too much. There was something that I meant to tell you, something I think that you should know.

"There was another one of you. Another synthetic man sent out on another ship . . ."

"Yes, I knew about that," said Blake. "I've often wondered—what do you know of him?"

"He came back," said the mind of Theodore Roberts. "Brought back. Much the same as you . . ."

"You mean suspended animation?"

"Yes. But this time the ship came home. A few years after it went out. The crew was frightened by what had happened and . . ."

"So I was no great surprise?"

"Yes, I am inclined to think you were. No one tied you up with what had happened so long ago. Not too many people in Space knew about it. It wasn't until shortly before you escaped from the hospital, after the bioengineering hearing, that anyone began to wonder if you might not be the other one. But before anything could be done about it, you had disappeared."

"This other one? He is still on Earth? Space had him?"

"I don't think so," said the mind of Theodore Roberts. "I don't really know. He disappeared. I know that much . . ."

"He disappeared! You mean they destroyed him!"

"I don't know."

"Damn it, you must know," screamed Blake. "Tell me! I'll go out there and tear the place apart. I'll find him . . ."

"It's no use," said Theodore Roberts. "He isn't there. Not any more."

"But when? How long ago?"

"Several years ago. Well before you were brought back from space."

"Look—how do you know? Who told you . . ."

"There are thousands of us here," said Theodore Roberts. "What one knows is available to all. There's little that one misses."

Blake felt the freezing breath of futility closing in upon him. The other man had disappeared, Theodore Roberts said, and undoubtedly he should know. But where? Dead? Hidden away somewhere? Sent out into space again?

The one man, the only other being in the universe to which he could have felt close kinship—and now that man was gone.

"You're sure?"

"I'm sure," said Theodore Roberts.

After a silence, Roberts asked, "You're going back to space? You have decided to?"

"Yes," said Blake. "Yes, I think I have. There's nothing here on Earth."

And there was, he knew, nothing here on Earth. If the other man was gone, there was nothing left on Earth. Elaine Horton had refused to talk with him and her father, once so friendly, had been cold and formal when he said good-bye, and Theodore Roberts was a frosty voice speaking from the emptiness of one dimension.

"When you come back," said Theodore Roberts, "I'll still be here. You will phone me, please. You will get in touch?"

If I come back, thought Blake. If you still are here. If there is anybody here. If Earth is worth the coming back to.

"Yes," he said. "Yes, of course, I'll phone you."

He reached out and flipped the toggle to break communication.

And sat, unstirring, in the dark and silence, feeling the Earth drawing back and away from him, flowing outward in an expanding circle that left him all alone.

35

Earth lay behind. The Sun had shrunk, but was still the Sun and not another star. The ship was falling down the long tunnel of gravitational vectors that would, in a little time, build up its velocity to the point where the stars would seem to start shifting in their courses and their colors and it then would begin its slow transition into that other universe which existed beyond the speed of light.

Blake sat in the pilot's chair, gazing through the curved transparency that opened out on space. It was so quiet here, he thought, so quiet and peaceful—the uneventfulness of the emptiness that lay between the stars. In a little while he'd have to get up and take a turn about the ship to satisfy himself that all was right and well, although he knew it would be. With a ship such as this nothing could go wrong.

—Going home, said Quester, speaking quietly in Blake's mind. Going home again.

—But not for long, Blake told him. Only long enough to pick up the data that we missed before—that you didn't have the time to get. Then moving on, to where you can reach out to other stars.

And going on and on, he thought, always moving on to harvest other stars, running the data gathered from them through the biological computer that was Thinker's mind. Seeking, ever seeking, for the hints and clues that would make the pattern of the universe fall into a framework of understanding. And what would they find? he wondered. Many things, perhaps, that no one now could suspect.

—Quester's wrong, said Thinker. We have no home. We cannot have a home. Changer found that out. In time we'll realize that we do not need a home.

—The ship will be our home, said Blake.

—Not the ship, said Thinker. If you insist upon a home, then the universe. All space is home to us. The entire universe.

And that, thought Blake, might have been in substance what the mind of Theodore Roberts had tried to say to him. Earth is no more than a point in space, he'd said. And so, of course, were all the other planets, all the other stars—only points of matter and of energy, concentrated in remote localities, with emptiness between. Intelligence, Roberts had said, is all there is; it's the one significance. Not life alone, not matter, not energy, but intelligence. Without intelligence, all this scattered matter, all the flaming energy, all the emptiness, was of no consequence because it did not have a meaning. It was only intelligence that could take the matter and the energy and make it meaningful.

Although, thought Blake, it would be good to have an anchor somewhere in all this emptiness, to be able to point, if only in one's mind, to a particular glob of energy, and say that is my home—to have a place to tie to, to possess some frame of reference.

He sat in his chair, staring out at space, remembering once again that moment in the chapel when he had sensed for the first time his basic homelessness—that he never could belong, not on Earth, not anywhere, that while of Earth he never could be of Earth, that while human in his form he never could be human. But that moment, he realized now, also had shown him that no matter how homeless he might be, he was not alone and could never be alone. He had the other two, and he had more than that. He had the universe and all the ideas, all the fantasies, all the seething intellectual ferment that had ever risen in it.

Earth could have been a home, he thought; he had a right to expect it could be home. A point in space, he thought. And that was right—Earth was a tiny point in space. But no matter how tiny it might be, man needed such a point as a homing signal, as a beacon. The universe was not enough because it was too much. As a man from Earth, one stood for something, possessed identity; but the man of the universe was lost among the stars.

He heard the soft fall of the footstep and sprang up and swung around.

Elaine Horton stood just inside the door.

He took a quick step forward, then halted, frozen in his tracks.

"No!" he shouted. "No! You don't know what you're doing."

A stowaway, he thought—a mortal on an immortal ship. And she had refused to talk with him, she'd . . .

"But I do," she said. "I do know what I'm doing. I'm where I belong."

"An android," he said in bitterness. "A simulated human. Sent to make me happy. While the real Elaine . . ."

"Andrew," she said, "I am the real Elaine."

He half lifted his arms, a gesture, and she suddenly was in them and he held her close, his body aching in happiness at her being there, at having someone human, at the closeness of a very special human.

"But, you can't!" he cried. "You can't. You don't realize what's going on. I'm not human. I'm not always this way. I turn into other things."

She lifted her head and looked at him. "But I know," she said. "You don't understand. I'm the other one—the other one of us."

"There was another man," he said, somewhat stupidly. "There was . . ."

"Not another man. A woman. The other was a woman."

And that was it, of course, he thought. Theodore Roberts, not knowing, had said the other man.

"But Horton? You are Horton's daughter."

She shook her head. "There was an Elaine Horton, but she died. Committed suicide. Rather horribly and for some sordid reason. It would have wrecked the senator's career."

"Then you . . ."

"That's right. Not that I knew anything about it. When the senator set out to dig up the facts about the old Project Werewolf, he had found out about me. He saw me and was struck by my resemblance to his daughter. Of course I was in suspended animation then, had been for years on end. We were very naughty people, Andrew. We did not turn out at all the way they thought we would."

"I know," he said. "I know. I'm a little glad right now we didn't. So you knew all the time . . ."

"Just recently," she said. "The senator, you see, had Space across the barrel. They wanted very much to keep the Werewolf business under wraps. So when he came to them, frantic with grief at his daughter's death, crazy at the thought he was a ruined man, they gave me to him. I thought I was his daughter. I loved him as my father. I had been brain-washed, conditioned, whatever it is that they do to you, to make me think that I was his daughter."

"He must have pulled a lot of weight. To hush up his daughter's death and then take you . . ."

"He was the one who could manage it," she declared. "He was a lovely man, such a lovely father—but ruthless when it came to politics."

"You loved him."

She nodded. "That's it, Andrew. In many ways, he still

is father to me. No one can ever guess what it took for him to tell me."

"And you?" he asked. "It cost you something, too."

"Don't you see," she said. "I couldn't stay. Once I knew, I simply couldn't stay. I would have been a freak, as much as you. Living on and on. And once the senator should die, what would be left for me?"

He nodded, understanding, thinking of two people, two humans, facing that decision.

"Besides," she said, "I belonged with you. I think I knew it from the first—from that moment you stumbled, all soaked and cold, into that old stone house."

"The senator told me . . ."

"That I didn't want to see you, that I didn't want to talk with you."

"But why?" he asked. "But why?"

"They were trying to scare you off," she said. "They were afraid you wouldn't go, that you'd try to cling to Earth. They wanted you to think there was nothing left for you on Earth. The senator and the mind of Theodore Roberts and all the rest of them. Because we had to go, you see. We are the instruments of Earth, the gift of the Earth to the universe. If the intelligences of the universe ever are to find out what is happening, what has happened, what will happen, what it's all about, we can help in the doing of it."

"Then we are of Earth? The Earth still claims us . . ."

"Of course," she said. "Now that they know about us, the Earth is proud of us."

He held her body close to his and knew that Earth finally was, and forever would be, home. That wherever they might go, humanity would be with them. For they were the extensions of humanity, the hand and mind of mankind reaching out into the mysteries of all eternity.

THE WORLD OF NULL-A

by A. E. VAN VOGT

"In A.D. 2560 Earth had become the world of Null-A, or non-Aristotelianism, controlled by a gigantic Games Machine, made up of twenty-five thousand electronic brains. . . . Gilbert Gosseyn came to the Games Machine that year, only to find that he didn't know who he was, and, even more amazing, that he could be killed and still live, in his own original body!

"Later, Gosseyn learned that he was evidently a pawn in an astral game some super-brain was playing to thwart an attack on the solar system from outer space. Mr. van Vogt's novel shuttles back and forth between Venus and Earth, and the story is packed with Hitchcockian action. . . . The science-fiction fan whose name has become legion in recent years, will hail it as the classic of the year."
—*New York Herald Tribune*

This edition specially revised
and with a new Introduction
by the author

A Berkley Medallion Book
(S1802—75¢)

RETIEF AND THE WARLORDS

by KEITH LAUMER

The lobster-like Haterakans—"Hatracks" to their enemies
(they had no friends)—were infiltrating human-held planets in the Goober Cluster—and Earth's response was to
offer them lots of foreign aid! When things get that skewed,
there's only one man for the job—that perpetual holder of
the short end of the stick, Jame Retief . . . and in *RETIEF
AND THE WARLORDS,* the galactic diplomat is at his
breeziest and most casually lethal, winding up his mission
in a slambang three-way showdown.

A Berkley Medallion Book
(X1800—60¢)

Send for a free list of all our books in print

These books are available at your local newsstand, or send
price indicated plus 10¢ per copy to cover mailing costs
to Berkley Publishing Corporation, 200 Madison Avenue,
New York, N.Y. 10016.

APEMAN, SPACEMAN

Anthropological Science Fiction

edited by LEON E. STOVER & HARRY HARRISON

What would happen if a galactic survey team picked an Eskimo as representative of Earth's highest form of civilization? If dolphins had to train man to survive in their world after the holocaust? If there were a lost tribe of Neanderthals somewhere?

These are just a few of the fascinating questions posed in this brilliant anthology, which traces man in fact and in fiction from his origins to an imagined future. Among the distinguished scientists, science fiction authors, and scientist-SF authors represented are Earnest A. Hooton, Carleton S. Coon, Harold D. Lasswell, Robert A. Heinlein, and Arthur C. Clarke.

A Berkley Medallion Book
(N1819—95¢)

BEST SF STORIES
FROM NEW WORLDS 3

edited by MICHAEL MOORCOCK

Michael Moorcock's *New Worlds* is recognized by many as
the most dynamic SF magazine in the world today.

Here is a vigorous trail-blazing magazine whose writers
carry you on voyages into the unknown—voyages which are
original, disturbing and above all, different.

The writers appearing in this volume are:

George Collyn
Brian W. Aldiss
Langdon Jones
Peter Tate
Charles Platt
Pamela Zoline
Keith Roberts
George MacBeth
James Sallis
P. F. Woods
James Colvin

A Berkley Medallion Book
(S1790—75¢)